A STO

Alex lifted her hand [...]
and sweet through the [...]
haps we should rejoin them?"

Georgina smiled. "Before your mother recalls her duties as chaperone and sends Emily out here to fetch us?"

"I doubt Mother would care if we stayed out here for hours," Alex laughed.

"Truly?" Georgina leaned just a bit closer to him, her hand still in his. "Then perhaps we should."

"Georgina." He stared down at her, his eyes shining and silvery. Then his arms came about her, warm and safe and sheltering. "Blast it all, Georgie, but I cannot be a gentleman one second longer."

His lips came down to meet hers. Georgina's eyes widened in surprise, then fluttered closed at the delicious warmth that flooded through her like fine brandy. She looped her arms around his neck, burying her fingers in his soft curls as his mouth slanted on hers. . . .

Lady Rogue

Amanda McCabe

A SIGNET BOOK

SIGNET
Published by New American Library, a division of
Penguin Putnam Inc., 375 Hudson Street,
New York, New York 10014, U.S.A.
Penguin Books Ltd, 80 Strand,
London WC2R 0RL, England
Penguin Books Australia Ltd, Ringwood,
Victoria, Australia
Penguin Books Canada Ltd, 10 Alcorn Avenue,
Toronto, Ontario, Canada M4V 3B2
Penguin Books (N.Z.) Ltd, 182–190 Wairau Road,
Auckland 10, New Zealand

Penguin Books Ltd, Registered Offices:
Harmondsworth, Middlesex, England

First published by Signet, an imprint of New American Library,
a division of Penguin Putnam Inc.

First Printing, February 2002
10 9 8 7 6 5 4 3 2 1

 REGISTERED TRADEMARK—MARCA REGISTRADA

Printed in the United States of America

PUBLISHER'S NOTE
This is a work of fiction. Names, characters, places, and incidents either are
the product of the author's imagination or are used fictitiously, and any resem-
blance to actual persons, living or dead, business establishments, events, or
locales is entirely coincidental.

BOOKS ARE AVAILABLE AT QUANTITY DISCOUNTS WHEN USED TO PROMOTE
PRODUCTS OR SERVICES. FOR INFORMATION PLEASE WRITE TO PREMIUM MAR-
KETING DIVISION, PENGUIN PUTNAM INC., 375 HUDSON STREET, NEW YORK, NEW
YORK 10014.

To Katie Fish, the "real" Lady Kate,
and to her parents, Hugh and Anita Fish,
for being three such wonderful friends.

Chapter One

"So that is it, then? That is all that is left?" Alexander Kenton, late of His Majesty's army and now the new Duke of Wayland, stared out of the library window at the bedraggled garden beyond. Yet he did not see the overgrown, rain-soaked bushes and trampled flower beds. He saw only the great tangle his life had suddenly become.

The solicitor, seated at the desk behind him, rattled papers and coughed uncomfortably. "I fear so, my lord."

Alex laughed bitterly. "Well. You have to admire a brother who can manage to leave such a thorough mess in such a brief time."

"Indeed, my lord," the solicitor answered, in a small, uncertain voice.

Alex pushed back from the window and returned to his seat before the fire, stretching his booted feet to its meager warmth. "Tell me, then, Mr. Reed, what we have to live on, Mother and Emily and me, once all of Damian's debts are settled."

Mr. Reed consulted his papers again. "Fair Oak, the house and the farm, of course. And the Kenton

Grange. Those are entailed. Aside from your personal belongings, and the few family jewels now in the possession of the dowager duchess, I fear there is little else."

"Emily's dowry?"

"Gone, my lord. Long gambled away."

"Damn," Alex cursed softly. "The farm has not been worked in years! Not since my father's time."

"I do believe that Lady Emily has managed to keep some of the fields under cultivation. Much of the land, though, has lain fallow since your late father's time. Your brother was not—not much interested in farming."

"Damian was not much interested in anything but gambling and whoring."

The solicitor blushed.

"Forgive my bluntness, Mr. Reed," Alex said. "Years in the army will do that to a man."

"Quite understandable, my lord."

"So, in effect, all we have to restore this old pile and give Emily a proper come-out is my army pension."

"There is a small income from the tenants still left, my lord, and Lady Dorothy has an annuity of her own. But, in essence, yes, you are right. I fear so." Mr. Reed gathered his papers together and stood. "If you have no further questions of me at this time, my lord, I will leave you to your supper."

"Yes, of course. Thank you, Mr. Reed."

Alex turned his gaze back to the flames as the library door clicked shut, leaving him alone with his thoughts.

They were not happy, tranquil thoughts.

"I should have stayed in the army," he muttered. "Spain and Belgium were simpler than this."

But then, with the war ended, there had been no point

in staying with the army. He had longed for home, for the green coolness of Fair Oak, for the company of his family. His excellent father had died almost five years ago, when Alex had been in the heat of the fighting. His older brother had died last year of a fall from a horse, during a race. Alex had not wanted to be the duke, but he had come home prepared to do his duty.

He had not known until just now how badly Damian had bungled things.

In less than five years, Damian had managed to gamble away a very comfortable fortune. He had spent so recklessly on mistresses, parties, horse races, and cards that everything that was not entailed had had to be sold to pay for them.

What was Alex to do now? He himself could live comfortably, if frugally, on his pension. His mother, though, was aging, and not in good health. His sister, who had held the household together for so long, deserved a fine Season, a good match. His ancestral home was collapsing about his ears. Even now, he could see plaster loosening from the ceiling, damp seeping down into the carpet and the draperies.

Yes, he should have stayed in Spain.

The library door opened, and Emily's golden-curled head popped inside. "Alex? Has Mr. Reed gone?"

Alex looked around at her, and smiled. Even in such dire circumstances, his sister could not fail to cheer him. She was a bouncing, elfin little thing, seemingly always laughing. Even in a faded, mended blue muslin frock, she shimmered.

"Yes, angel-puss, he has gone."

She came and sat in the chair next to his, stretching her own feet to the fire. "It is very bad, is it not?"

Alex could not lie to her. Not when she turned her wide, guileless blue gaze onto him. "Yes."

Emily sighed. "I knew it. I had hoped, though, that there would be something. Even Farmer Ellis, who sells us our butter and eggs, won't want to give us credit any longer!"

"What do you know about butter and eggs, angel?" Alex laughed.

Emily's lips pursed. "A great deal as it happens, brother. Our housekeeper left above six months ago, and someone had to deal with such things. Mother is not able."

Alex grew somber again. "I am sorry, Em. You should not have had to take on such tasks."

"I do not mind. But now I shall not have to, as you are here, and will no doubt conceive a great plan for our salvation!"

"I do not have a plan as yet, Em," he warned. "Damian left us in a very great mess, and it will take time to sort it out."

"Hm, yes. He was very naughty. Not at all like you, Alex."

"You do not think me naughty?" he teased.

"Of course not, how could you be? You have all those medals for bravery, and valor, and good deeds, and who knows what else. Earning all those would not have left you much time for anything else."

He laughed. "Quite right!"

A companionable silence fell between them. They sat and listened to the crackle of the fire, to the soft patter of the rain hitting the windows.

Then Alex said, "You may have to wait until next year for your Season, Em."

She shrugged. "I like it here at Fair Oak. Much more than I would in London, I'm sure. Who needs balls and routs?" Her face was wistful, despite her lighthearted words.

"You must have a proper Season!"

"So I shall. When things are better for us." A bell rang out from the direction of the drawing room, and Emily rose and smoothed her skirt. "That will be Mother, summoning us to supper. Thank goodness Cook is still with us! I fear I would be quite hopeless in the kitchen."

Alex caught her hand in his, and kissed it gently. "Things *will* be better for us soon, Em. I promise."

She smiled down at him. "I know. *You* are with us now; how bad could things be?" The bell rang again. "But come. Mother will be becoming impatient."

As Alex took her arm and led her from the library, she said, "What will you do now?"

"I think, sister dear, that I will go to London. Perhaps the solution to our troubles is there!"

Chapter Two

"Does it always rain in London?" Mrs. Georgina Beaumont leaned her forehead against the cool glass of the morning room window, watching the endless silvery sheets falling down on the small, beautifully manicured garden.

Lady Elizabeth Hollingsworth, seated before the fire with her feet up and a blanket tucked about her cozily, laughed.

Georgina's new dog, Lady Kate, a small white terrier Georgina had saved from being drowned by a farmer in Scotland, looked up at the sound of laughter. Then she yawned, stretched out on her satin cushion beside the fire, and went back to sleep. For once she was not barking and running about like a tiny bedlamite.

"Georgie," Elizabeth said. "It rains just as much in Venice as it does here."

"Hm. But it seems a much *warmer* rain there. Romantic. Here it is merely dreary."

"Then come away from the window, and sit here by the fire. What do you think we should do this evening? The Beaton ball? The Carstairs musicale?"

Georgina left the window and sat down on a settee next to the fire. She eyed Elizabeth worriedly. "Should you not stay home tonight, Lizzie? We were out so very late last night."

"I am *enceinte*, not ill!" Elizabeth protested. "I am barely showing as yet. I must have fun while I can, before I grow as big as a house." She tugged the blanket aside to peer down at her belly, only a bit rounded beneath her pale green morning dress.

Georgina laughed at the vision of her petite friend as round as a full moon, waddling about Bond Street. "I shall have to paint your portrait when that happens!"

"Don't you dare!" Elizabeth protested. "But I promise that if I grow fatigued I will say so. And no doubt you, under Nicholas's orders, will drag me home immediately."

"What a proud papa Nicholas is becoming! I vow one would think he had done it all himself, the way he has been preening about."

Elizabeth smiled softly at the mention of her husband. "Yes, he will be an excellent father. It seems we have waited an age for this, and now it is upon us!"

"I am so happy for you, Lizzie."

"Well, you, I am sure, will be the most excellent of godmothers."

"Oh, yes! I shall teach him or her to paint pictures and run wild."

"You will teach them to be true to themselves, to enjoy life. Those are the most valuable lessons of all, you know."

Georgina's laughter sounded a bit sad, even to her own ears. After three marriages, she remained childless. She had thought it all for the best; her life as an artist, racketing about the Continent, was not a very stable one. But now, seeing her friend's radiance, she could not help but be a bit regretful.

"Well, it was very good of you to come stay with me now, Georgie," Elizabeth continued. "I know how you miss Italy."

"I would not miss this time with you for the world! Besides, we are having a marvelous time, are we not?"

"We are! I am only vexed that Nicholas will not let me ride with you in that curricle race next week."

"*I* would not have let you in any case! You can watch safely from the side of the road as I trounce that arrogant Lord Pynchon."

"And I will make a great deal of money from wagering on you!" Elizabeth turned her head as a single ray of yellow-white light fell from the window across the carpet. "I do believe it has stopped raining! Shall we go out? I need to visit the lending library."

Lady Kate sat straight up, her ears perking at the mention of the word "out." She leaped off of her cushion and trotted over to the cabinet where her leads were kept, barking her sharp "go for a walk" bark.

"I think Lady Kate is in agreement," said Georgina. "We should take her for a run in the park, as well."

"What a good idea! And let us call at my brother's house and see if my niece Isabella would like to accompany us. We could take her to Gunter's for ices after. She is rather lonely, with Peter and Carmen still on their wedding trip."

"Oh, yes, let's! We shall make a day of it."

The first thing Alex saw was the hat.

It was wide-brimmed, fine-milled straw, with fluttering streamers of pale green and white satin. Perhaps not precisely appropriate for London in early spring, but certainly fetching.

Then his gaze lowered to the lady beneath the hat, and he very nearly fell from his saddle in startled admiration. She was—well, she was very *vivid*. Quite a contrast to the giggling young misses his friends had taken to hurling in his direction since his return to London.

She was not very tall, but her posture, her manner of walking, made her seem almost Amazonian. She wore a pelisse of a green that matched the streamers of her hat, and the hair that fell from beneath that hat could only be described as red. Not a fashionable auburn, or a demure dark blonde, but the very red and gold of flames. Or—or a sunset.

Good gad, man, he berated himself. *You're beginning to sound like some deuced poet!*

Yet if he were to turn to poetry, surely a woman like this one would be all that was needed to inspire him.

She was strolling alongside the river with a petite female companion and a little girl. Looped about her gloved wrist was the braided lead of a small white dog, who was darting about in a most unpredictable manner and barking at every unsuspecting passerby. The woman laughed merrily at the dog's antics. Not a ladylike simper or giggle, but a full, deep, rich, laugh.

Alex could not help but smile at the infectious sound of it.

"Why, Freddie! I do believe Wayland is ogling La Beaumont."

Alex's two companions, his old Etonian friends Mr. Freddie Marlow and Hildebrand Rutherford, Viscount Garrick, pulled up their horses on either side of Alex's, and followed his gaze to its object.

"I say, I do believe you are right, Hildebrand! What excellent taste you show, Wayland. Mrs. Beaumont is extraordinary. Though, I must say I rather prefer her friend, Lady Elizabeth Hollingsworth, myself. I always had a weakness for pocket Venuses!"

Alex scarcely glanced at his friends. The dog and the little girl were walking down to the edge of the river, and the two women followed. A breeze threatened to carry away that fanciful hat, and she clutched at it with one gloved hand.

"The woman with the red hair is a Mrs. Beaumont?" he asked.

"Mrs. Georgina Beaumont, the artist. Surely you have heard of her?" said Freddie.

Alex feared he knew little about art. Or artists. "Is she married?"

"A widow!" Hildebrand said with a certain glee. "Three times over. That is even better, eh? Good sport, what?"

Alex turned a glare onto him, and Hildebrand stifled his chortles behind a gloved hand.

"As I said, she is an artist," offered Freddie. "A deuced successful one, from what I hear, though I'm a complete bacon-brain about painting and music and such."

"She's come from her home in Italy to stay for the Season with Lady Elizabeth," said Hildebrand, now recovered from his giggling fit. "It's quite the fashion to be in love with one or the other of them. Though Lady Elizabeth *is* married, more is the pity."

A thrice-married artist. Alex almost laughed at the thought of the looks on his family's faces if he brought such a woman home to the Grange! Not, of course, that Mother and Em were such high sticklers as all *that*.

They just maintained certain standards, despite their straitened circumstances.

But then, Alex had always had a great weakness for red hair.

He looked from one of his friends to the other speculatively. "I take it, then, that one of you has been introduced to the lady?"

"I haven't," Freddie said, his wide brown eyes looking positively downcast at this fact. "Hildebrand has."

"At Lady Russell's card party a fortnight ago," Hildebrand preened. "Should you like me to do the honors, Wayland?"

Alex gave him a long look, and Hildebrand coughed uncomfortably. "Er, yes," he said. "Just so. Most happy to perform the introductions, I'm sure."

They had only just turned their horses in the direction of the ladies, when disaster struck.

The small white dog, who had been regularly menacing any and all unwary pedestrians, now broke free from the lead the little girl held, and bounded away down the riverbank after an errant duck. In a swift white blur, it became airborne, and landed with a great splash in the murky river. Only its pale head was visible as it drifted off, carried inexorably away by the current.

"Lady Kate!" Mrs. Beaumont cried. She lifted her skirts indecently high above her ankles, revealing green kid half boots and an inch of white stocking, and dashed off after her dog. Her hat fell from her head to dangle down her back by its ribbons.

The little girl followed, shouting, "Be careful, Georgie! You'll fall in the river!"

The petite woman, Lady Elizabeth, ran after the girl, crying out, "Help! Help!" to no one in particular.

Mrs. Beaumont nearly slid down in the mud at the edge of the river, tottering precariously on those half boots. "Lady Kate! Come back, darling!"

Alex was already sliding from his saddle, and striding away across a busy thoroughfare and a wide greensward that separated him from the rather bizarre party of ladies.

He had faced many a dire situation in Spain, when he had had to think and act quickly, decisively, and calmly. To be sure, he had never seen a situation quite like this one in Spain, but he knew at a glance what had to be done to save the dog.

He stripped off his coat and boots, pushed them into the arms of the beauteous Mrs. Beaumont, and jumped in after the dog.

Georgina watched in astonishment as the man—a man she had never seen before in her life!—dove into the murky waters after the escaping Lady Kate.

It had all happened so very quickly that she felt all in a daze. One moment she had been strolling along with Elizabeth and little Isabella, laughing and enjoying the day. Lady Kate had been frisking about, as usual; she was quite the most curious and excitable dog Georgina had ever seen. Then, all at once, Lady Kate had twisted out of her lead, scampered down to the river, and splashed right in!

And the man, whose coat and boots Georgina now held, had appeared seemingly out of nowhere and gone in after Lady Kate. Like some sun-bronzed guardian angel.

Georgina bit her lip in anxiety as she watched the man seize Lady Kate about her torso and pull her along toward the bank. The dog struggled mightily in his grasp, howling and frightened that her adventure had ended so badly, but the man hung grimly on. Finally, they both stood before Georgina, dripping with great quantities of dirty water but safely on *terra firma*.

"I believe, madam," the man said, his voice brandy-rich, rough with laughter, "that this belongs to you."

Georgina laughed, hiccuped really, with embarrassment and consternation and a dawning realization of the utter absurdity of their situation. "Yes, indeed, it does! Thank you so much, sir. You have gone quite above and beyond the call of gallantry! I do not believe I can thank you enough."

"He is a *hero*, Georgie," little Isabella Everdean piped up. She gazed up at their rescuer with adoring chocolate-brown eyes.

Georgina very much feared she was doing the same. Gaping at him like the veriest moonstruck half-wit! It was just that he was so very *beautiful*, even dripping with mud and odd plant life, his light brown, curling hair plastered to his head. Her artist's eye skimmed over his high cheekbones and firm jaw, lightly shadowed with afternoon whiskers. His nose was straight as a knife blade; his lips firm but strangely sensual. And his eyes, alight with laughter, were a clear, sweet, heavenly blue.

And they were looking directly into hers as she gaped at him.

She looked down, startled. Which was not at all like her! She was never startled by any man; she had met too many, had married three, and been propositioned by a numberless horde. She had thought herself rather *blasé* about men.

This one, though, had her *blushing*. She could feel the heat creeping up her throat into her cheeks, no doubt clashing horribly with her hair.

Elizabeth was looking at her rather peculiarly, so

Georgina knew that her odd behavior was not going unnoticed.

She forced her gaze back up to meet his, and she smiled. "How very rag-mannered you must think us, not even introducing ourselves after your heroic actions! I am Mrs. Georgina Beaumont."

He bowed, rather awkwardly with his arms full of wriggling terrier. "Alexander Kenton, at your service."

"And this is Lady Elizabeth Hollingsworth and Lady Isabella Everdean, her niece," Georgina continued.

"Lady Elizabeth, Lady Isabella." He bowed again in their direction. "How do you do."

Isabella giggled.

"Bella," Elizabeth chided. "Say how do you do."

"How d'ye do," said Isabella.

"It was so good of you to rescue Lady Kate," Elizabeth said. "I have told Georgina that she needs a stronger lead."

"You may be assured she will now have one!" Georgina snorted.

"May I carry Lady Kate now?" beseeched Isabella, going up on tiptoe to pat the muddy dog.

"You will get your frock all dirty!" cried Elizabeth.

"Why don't we wrap her in my coat?" Alexander suggested. "Then perhaps I could escort you to your carriage, and make certain she is safely stowed aboard?"

"Oh!" Only then did Georgina notice the interested crowd they had gathered. Many a quizzing glass was turned in her direction, and two gentlemen in particular, a Viscount Garrick she had already met and a man she had not, had edged their horses in closer to their little scene.

Ah, well. Georgina shrugged philosophically; she was quite used to people gawking at her escapades.

"You *have* gotten yourself into a scrape, Wayland!" said Viscount Garrick.

Alexander frowned at him, and shifted Lady Kate in his arms.

Elizabeth looked over at the two horsemen. "Are they with you, sir?"

"Unfortunately, yes," Alex murmured.

"Well, then, you must all come to my house for tea! We will have you dry and warm in a trice, sir. I am certain my husband will have some garments you could borrow."

"That is very kind of you, Lady Elizabeth, but . . ." Alex began.

Elizabeth lifted her hand, forestalling all protests. "No, I do insist! We want to thank you properly. Is that not so, Georgina?"

Elizabeth smiled at Alexander, and, slowly, like sun coming from behind the clouds, he smiled back. "Quite so, Elizabeth." Georgina said. "Quite so."

Chapter Three

Georgina had been wrong about Alexander Kenton. He was not beautiful.

He was otherworldly.

Dry and clean, his hair was a light brown, tinged gold by the sun. Tiny lines radiated out from the corners of his eyes, which were vividly blue against the bronze of his skin, every time he laughed. His shoulders were very broad beneath his borrowed coat, and his bearing was quite poised and straight and correct. He must have been in the army, like her first husband, Jack.

Georgina thought he looked like a Caravaggio painting.

He was also a duke.

A frown pulled at her brow at the thought. *That* was a bit problematic. Peers, especially dukes, seemed the very worst of lechers, always cornering her in dim corridors or dark garden bowers, always thinking she would be full of gratitude for their ham-handed attentions. Her trusty sharp-tipped hair ornaments had quickly disabused them all of such notions.

She would have so hated to use one on this particular duke!

But thus far there seemed no danger of that. Alexander Kenton was a very charming duke. He had taken the entire Lady Kate situation with such good humor, as no other man of her acquaintance would have done. He even fed the dog, now dry and clean and not a bit sorry for all the trouble she had caused, bits of his tea cakes and sandwiches. He conversed with Isabella quite as if she were grown-up. He laughed and joked, and did not once try to flirt with Georgina in any but the lightest and most respectful way.

His two friends, Viscount Garrick and Mr. Marlow, were a bit sillier. They told horrifyingly bad jokes, and obviously thought themselves quite the wits for it. Occasionally, one or the other would cast her provocative glances. Or rather, they would simply roll their eyes and wiggle their eyebrows in what they obviously fancied passed as provocative ways.

But Alexander; ah, now, he could easily prove far too attractive for her own good.

". . . Is that not so, Georgina?"

Georgina's attention snapped back to Elizabeth, from whence it had wandered into the clouds. "I beg your pardon?"

Elizabeth's gray eyes were slate dark with concern. "Are you quite all right, dear? You look flushed. Did you catch a chill by the river?"

"Indeed not! I am quite well. It should be Lord Wayland we are concerned about catching chills."

Alexander laughed. "Not I, Mrs. Beaumont! I am healthy as a horse."

"Perhaps I should give you both a dose of castor oil," Elizabeth mused.

"No!" Georgina and Alexander both shouted.

Lady Kate barked riotously, quite as if she also had been offered a dose.

"You must forgive Elizabeth," Georgina said. "She feels it her bounden duty to nurse and cosset everyone who comes into her sphere."

"Indeed I do not!" Elizabeth protested.

"You must remain healthy for this evening, Wayland," Freddie Marlow said. "You would not want to miss Lady Beaton's ball."

"We are also attending the Beaton ball!" said Elizabeth.

"It is predicted to be a dreadful crush," Freddie answered, obviously delighted at the prospect.

"It always is. It is simply a great pity that my husband is in the country this week and will have to miss it!"

Georgina glanced at Alexander over the rim of her teacup. "Perhaps we shall see you there, then, Lord Wayland. That is, if you have not caught a chill."

He grinned at her. His smile was very wide and white against his tanned skin. "I could wish the same for you, Mrs. Beaumont. But perhaps you would allow me to escort you and Lady Elizabeth to the ball? In the absence of your husband, Lady Elizabeth."

Yes, yes, yes! Georgina's mind shouted. Aloud she said, "How very kind of you! Have we not imposed on you quite enough for one day?"

"Nonsense! I have not had so much fun since I returned to England. Please, do allow me to escort you."

Georgina exchanged a look with Elizabeth, and nodded. "Then, we would be honored. And I promise you, we will leave Lady Kate at home!"

Alexander laughed. "I thank you for that! I should

so hate to have to fish Lady Kate out of Lady Beaton's Italian fountain."

"Why, Wayland! You sly rogue," Hildebrand exclaimed as they rode away from Lady Elizabeth's house. "You have solved all your difficulties most neatly, all in one afternoon."

Alex frowned. He would never have told anyone of his family's troubles, if he could help it; crying of misfortunes was not at all his style. But Hildebrand and Freddie had been his friends since they were boys, and when they had come upon him completely foxed one day after dealing with five of Damian's creditors, he had told them everything.

Yet Alex could not see that anything much had been solved by their afternoon. They had had a very nice tea with three very lovely ladies—one lovely, red-headed lady in particular. He had also ruined a quite fine coat by wrapping it about a muddy dog; a coat he could ill-afford to replace at present.

He expressed this to his friends, and added, "How tea and a ruined coat can solve my troubles, I fear I could not say, Hildebrand. Perhaps you would enlighten me?"

"You nodcock! Don't try and cozen me. I saw how bent you were on charming Mrs. Beaumont."

Alex shrugged. "She is a very beautiful woman."

"And a very *rich* one! She has widow's portions from three husbands, as well as a rather handsome income from her dabbling in painting."

"She is perhaps not entirely *respectable*—not with the highest sticklers, anyway," Freddie chimed in. "Racketing all over the Continent by herself."

"All the better!" said Hildebrand. "She wouldn't

expect you to live in her pocket. You could do worse, Wayland."

Alex was so startled he pulled up his horse right in the middle of the road, causing quite a muddle of the traffic behind them. He stared at his friends, his jaw tight with displeasure. "Are you suggesting," he said very quietly, "that I pursue Mrs. Beaumont for her money?"

Hildebrand sputtered. "Why . . . is that not what you were thinking of?"

"It could not be Lady Elizabeth," Freddie said. " 'Old Nick' Hollingsworth is an absolute jealous fiend when it comes to his beloved wife."

"I was not thinking of either of those ladies in such a way," Alex answered, still quiet.

"Oh, well, I just thought . . . when you offered to escort them to the Beaton ball . . . but I . . ." Hildebrand broke off in a state of utter confusion.

"Oh, look!" cried Freddie in relief. "Here is Wayland's lodgings."

"Indeed it is!" Hildebrand replied, in equal relief. "Well, we shall leave you, then, Wayland. See you at the ball, what?"

Then the two of them dashed off, leaving Alex alone in front of the narrow town house, where he rented the second floor while he was in London. Clifton House in Grosvenor Square had been lost long ago by Damian.

He left his horse at the mews at the foot of the garden, and went up to his small sitting room to pour himself a brandy and settle in for a good brood.

He, marry that lovely Mrs. Beaumont for her money? Distasteful in the extreme.

Not that he had not thought at all of marrying for money. Really, in the eyes of many, it would be an eminently suitable solution. A wife of means could not only restore Fair Oak, buy a new proper London house, and finance Emily's launch; she could also guide that launch and help Emily make a good match.

The wife, of course, in turn, would get to be the Duchess of Wayland. Not a shabby return on investment, some would say. He had even noticed many women eyeing him speculatively at balls and routs.

Alex had made and discarded many other, less feasible plans to recoup his family's losses. Some, made in the midst of sleepless nights, had been positively bizarre. He had half made up his mind to look about this Season for someone suitable. Not a young miss, but perhaps someone older, a spinster or a widow. Someone kind and practical, who understood what was expected of her in the marriage and what she could expect in return. Someone he could be friends with; perhaps even admire.

Someone like—Georgina Beaumont.

Alex tossed back his brandy, and reached out to pour himself another.

He truly had not thought of such a thing when he met her that afternoon. He had heard of her, of course; every lady of fashion clamored to have her portrait painted by Mrs. Beaumont. No doubt they paid handsomely for the privilege.

But all he had thought when he saw her was how lovely she was, how vibrant, how confident, how *alive*.

After years of the dust, death, and boredom of war, followed by the strain of his family's situation, that vivid life had been intoxicating. He had been drawn to her, as to a roaring fire on a bitterly cold winter night. He had wanted to stay longer in her presence, to throw aside the polite platitudes they were actually voicing and ask her how she came to be an artist. Did she enjoy living in Italy; did she love her husbands? What did she like to eat for breakfast?

Would she let him sit near her and kiss her, just once?

Alex laughed bitterly at himself. She, no doubt, would find him a very dull fellow. A military man, crusty and cynical, with no deep knowledge of art, could not possibly interest a woman such as her.

If he were to make her such an offer, the use of her money for the use of his title, she would no doubt treat it with the contempt it deserved, and laugh him from the room.

But . . .

But if she *were* his wife, he could make love to her. Maybe even more than once.

"Alex, you old idiot," he remonstrated aloud. "You have spent far too many years in the Spanish sun. Your brain is baked for even thinking such thoughts of a woman you met only two hours ago!"

And he had gone his own way for too long. He could not rely on a woman to solve his difficulties now.

A soft knock sounded at his door. Alex, so caught up in visions of Georgina Beaumont, thought for one insane instant that perhaps it was she at the door. Then reality returned, and he sank back into his chair.

No doubt it was some other creditor of Damian's, come to collect his due.

"Enter," he called out, suddenly weary beyond belief.

Yet it was not creditors. It was Hildebrand and Freddie, looking equal parts wary and shamefaced.

"I thought you two were going home to change for the ball," he told them. "What brings you back to my humble abode?"

At his easy tone, they broke into smiles, coming into the room to seat themselves and help themselves to the brandy.

"We came to apologize," said Freddie.

"Apologize?"

"For our—misconceptions of your intentions toward Mrs. Beaumont," Hildebrand said. "We truly didn't mean to offend, Wayland. Just want to be of assistance, looking about for suitable heiresses and such."

"What we really want," Freddie added, "is to find *three* heiresses, one for each of us."

"But a man is lucky to find one such in a Season," sighed Hildebrand. "So when we find her, we shall concede her to you."

"Very kind of you." Alex laughed. *Now* he remembered why he was still friends with these two after all these years, despite their silliness—they could always make him laugh.

"Yes. But we can see now that you are absolutely right about Mrs. Beaumont."

"Am I? How so?" Alex said, still laughing.

"She would be most unsuitable. Despite all her money, she is so dashed independent," answered Freddie. "Living alone in Italy and all. They say she even works with *male* models there!"

"Does she indeed?" said Alex, growing more interested by the moment.

"She is going to race her curricle against Lord Pynchon next week," Freddie said. "The betting book at White's is full of nothing else."

"What are the odds now?" asked Hildebrand.

"Three to one, in her favor."

"Hmm. There, you see, Wayland?" Hildebrand said. "She would not be a good duchess at all."

"She probably would not have him at all," commented Freddie. "She has often said she intends never to marry again. If he *did* make her an offer, she would no doubt turn him down flat."

Hildebrand nodded sagely. "No doubt you are right, Freddie."

Alex looked at them in astonishment. "Are you suggesting that if I made an offer to Mrs. Beaumont—which I have no intention of doing!—she would not see the advantages of it? That she would turn me down flat?"

Hildebrand and Freddie looked at each other. "Yes," they chorused.

"Hmph," said Alex.

Hildebrand shook his head. "But then, you are a handsome fellow. The ladies giggle over you wherever we go. Even Miss Pym has dropped poor Freddie quite flat since you appeared and danced with her at the Merritt rout."

"Here, now . . ." Freddie began, only to fall back silent at a glance from Hildebrand.

"Mrs. Beaumont seemed rather taken by you," Hildebrand continued. "She did not even laugh at my jokes! Perhaps she would be tempted by your own self, even if she has no desire to be a duchess. What do you think, Freddie?"

Freddie, still stung by the reminder of the defection of Miss Pym, said, "I still say she would have none of him."

"Well, I say she would!" cried Hildebrand. "I wager you fifty pounds they will be betrothed by the end of the Season."

"Done!" answered Freddie.

They looked expectantly to Alex, who raised his hands in mock surrender. "Do not look at me! I want nothing to do with any of your ridiculous wagers. Besides, I have only just met Mrs. Beaumont; the two of you are being extremely presumptuous."

Hildebrand smiled smugly. "We shall see, Wayland."

Chapter Four

"Lord Wayland is very handsome, is he not?"

Georgina looked up from brushing her hair at her dressing table over to where Elizabeth was sprawled across Georgina's chaise. Elizabeth was already dressed for the evening, in a lovely pale blue silk, but she was eating a box of sweets, and the sugary, sticky smears threatened her lace-trimmed bodice.

Lady Kate was fast asleep on the bed, utterly exhausted after all her adventures.

"Lizzie," said Georgina, "were those four cakes at tea not enough for you?"

"I know, I know! I could scarce lace myself into this gown as it is, but I cannot quite forgo eating sweets. The babe must be a girl. My old nanny always said women bearing sons craved salty foods, daughters sweets. But you are quite avoiding my question."

"Oh? Which question is that?"

"The question of whether you prefer lobster patties or goose liver paté, of course," Elizabeth scoffed. "It is the question of whether or not you consider Lord Wayland the handsomest man we have come across so far this Season! Excepting my darling Nick, of course."

Georgina drew the mass of her curly hair up off her neck and turned her head this way and that, studying the effect in the mirror. She was hesitating, and that was not at all like her. Usually she and Elizabeth chattered endlessly about anything and everything, from difficulties with their art and their careers to their romances (until Elizabeth married, that is!). Now, though, she did not want to *talk* about Lord Wayland; she only wanted to *think* about him for a while.

Why should that be?

She dropped her hair, and smiled at Elizabeth's reflection in the mirror. "I did not notice," she said indifferently.

"You! Not notice a gentleman's handsomeness, or lack thereof?" Elizabeth cried around a mouthful of sweet. "Ha! You are an artist, Georgie. It would be positively unprofessional of you not to notice."

Georgina smiled wryly. "You know me too well, Lizzie. Yes, Lord Wayland is quite handsome. By far the handsomest man we have met this year. Much more handsome than that Lord Percy, who every young miss has been sighing over."

"Hm, quite. Lord Percy is a young puppy, who lacks distinction. Unlike Lord Wayland. And those blue eyes . . ." Elizabeth sighed.

"Lizzie! You are a married woman."

"So I am," Elizabeth said unrepentantly. "And a very happy and faithful one, too, as unfashionable as that is. But you are not married, Georgie."

"No, and I intend to remain in that blissful state."

"Hm. Suit yourself." Elizabeth shrugged. "No one ever said you had to *marry* Lord Wayland. Just—be friends with him."

Georgina laughed. "Lizzie! You utter rogue!"

"I? A rogue? Oh, no, dear. I fear you claimed that title long ago. Lady Rogue!"

"Lady Rogue?" Georgina rather liked that. She preened a bit in the mirror, pursing her lips and batting her lashes. She and Elizabeth giggled. "Well, this rogue would like to be alone now, so she can bathe and change for the evening."

"Of course." Elizabeth stood up, and crossed the room to kiss Georgina's cheek before leaving, still in firm possession of the box of sweets. "You will want to look beautiful for Lord Wayland!"

Georgina shook her head at her friend's retreating figure, then turned her attention back to the mirror, reaching for her enameled powder pot. She had never considered herself beautiful, or even pretty. Her slanting green eyes were too widely spaced; there was a sprinkle of freckles across her too-small nose. And her hair, the despair of her youth, had never been any color but *red*. So unfashionable.

Yet she knew, without vanity, that many considered her beautiful. She had a hard-won air of confidence in herself, a fearless carriage that gave off such false impressions of height and loveliness. She liked that; it increased her fame and furthered her career. Yet *she* did not think herself beautiful at all.

She wondered if Lord Wayland thought her so.

For she certainly thought *him* beautiful. Those sun-touched brown curls and brilliant blue eyes would be such a joy to paint.

He was kind, as well. No other man, with the exception of Elizabeth's Nicholas, would have jumped into a muddy river after Lady Kate like that. And afterward, when other men would have railed about ruined pantaloons and the undoing of neck cloths, he had laughed. He had treated it all as a lark, as one of those silly, strange adventures that could beset one in the course of life.

"What a very unusual man," Georgina murmured. She fiddled with a scent bottle, lifting and dropping the jeweled stopper aimlessly as she thought about this man and their most strange meeting.

She wondered if he would like to have his portrait painted. In thanks for saving Lady Kate, of course.

Her musings were interrupted by the arrival of Daisy, Elizabeth's lady's maid, and two footmen bearing the bath.

"Oh! Now, just look at you, Mrs. B.," Daisy cried. "You've not even begun to get ready, and the carriage is ordered for nine."

"I am sorry, Daisy. I was woolgathering."

"I see that. Well, you just get in your bath, and I'll see about getting your gown pressed and ready." Daisy threw open the vast wardrobe and rifled through the myriad of colorful silks, satins, and muslins hanging there. "Which gown would you like to wear?"

"Oh, I don't know, Daisy. Something very dashing, I think!"

"Well, I think we won't have any problem finding something like *that*, Mrs. B.!"

It was a much-sobered Alex that presented himself on the Hollingsworth doorstep at half-past eight, immaculately attired for the evening. He bore a bouquet of roses for Lady Elizabeth, and a very large mass of very expensive orchids for Mrs. Beaumont.

He looked down now at the large purple blooms guiltily. They could be nothing but an apology, albeit a feeble one, for even thinking of—whatever it was he had been thinking of.

He almost turned and left, sure his guilt must show on his face for all to see, when he was forestalled by the butler answering his knock.

Lady Elizabeth was waiting for him in the drawing room, seated beside the fire. Alex had the fleeting, distracting thought that those flames were the exact color of Mrs. Beaumont's hair.

Elizabeth coughed delicately to catch his attention, and said, "Good evening, Lord Wayland."

Alex bowed quickly. "Good evening, Lady Elizabeth."

"Are those lovely flowers for us?"

"Indeed they are." He handed her the pink roses. "I know it is more the usual thing to send posies *after* a ball, but I wanted to thank you and Mrs. Beaumont for your kind hospitality this afternoon."

"You wish to thank *us*?" a voice cried behind him. "We should be the ones thanking you, Lord Wayland!"

Alex turned, and saw Georgina just entering the drawing room, fastening an emerald bracelet over one gloved wrist. He had read about one's breath "catching" in one's throat, but he had never experienced it before. Now he found that it was exactly as described; his breath lodged halfway up his throat and refused to pass any farther.

His impressions of that afternoon had been entirely correct, and not his imagination at all. Georgina Beaumont was a stunning woman. She wore a gown of brilliant green satin, draped low across her shoulders and, he couldn't help but notice, across her magnificent bosom. The gown was embroidered with gold thread on the bodice and along the hem; tiny emeralds winked amid the embroidery.

More emeralds swung at her ears, and her hair was drawn up and crowned with an emerald and topaz tiara of an unusual, spiked design—Russian, no doubt.

That tiara would probably keep Fair Oak going for a year.

Yet Alex did not see the splendor of her jewels. He saw only that she was lovely, that her smile was warm and wide and sincere as she greeted him. Unlike the silly simpers and smirks that had greeted him since he arrived in Town.

Her smile did not say, "Oh, grand, here is a *duke*." It said only that she was happy to see him.

He hoped.

"We should be thanking you," she continued as she advanced into the room and paused at his side. "Not one man in a hundred would have done as you did. You saved Lady Kate's life."

Alex's breath released then, and he was able to reply. "It was entirely my pleasure, ma'am. I have been quite a useless fribble since I returned to England; I was glad to have a mission again. I trust that, er, Lady Kate has suffered no ill effects from her swim?"

"Indeed not. I am happy to say that she is quite recovered."

As if summoned by the sound of her name, Lady Kate came bounding through the drawing room door. She took one glance at Alex, and dashed to his side, dancing up on her hind legs in order to plant her front paws on his immaculate breeches. She grinned in doggie delight.

"Oh, no!" Georgina cried. "Lady Kate, do get down from there!"

"I thought you had shut her in your room for the night, Georgie," said Elizabeth.

"I did, but she must have escaped. She does so hate to be excluded from any excitement. Come away, Lady Kate!"

"It's quite all right, Mrs. Beaumont." Alex leaned down to pat Lady Kate on the head and rub her silky ears. "I like animals very much. When I was a lad, I had a dog much like this one, but it was black."

Georgina watched as Lady Kate's stubby tail quivered in ecstasy. Such an effect this man had on females, both of the human and the canine persuasion! "Most of her type of terrier are black, I believe," she answered distractedly.

"However did you come across a white one, then, Mrs. Beaumont?"

"She saved Lady Kate from certain doom!" Elizabeth cried.

"Indeed?" Alex looked up at Georgina. "I should love to hear the tale of the rescue—the *first* rescue— of this admirable lady."

Georgina laughed. "It is not a very engrossing tale! Elizabeth, Nicholas, and I were on holiday in Scotland last autumn, when we came across a farmer about to drown a poor pup, because she was white."

"A horrid man!" said Elizabeth. "He said the 'wee beastie' was of no use, because she was too bright to be hidden from the game she was meant to be hunting."

"Yes," said Georgina. "She looked at me so imploringly. I could not leave her to her fate, so I bought her from the farmer for a shilling."

"A well-spent shilling, I would say," said Alex.

"I think so. Though you might not think her quite

so 'admirable,' if you were to look down now and see her eating your flowers!"

Alex looked, and saw that Lady Kate was indeed munching on an orchid. He laughed, and held the bedraggled bouquet out to Georgina. "Actually, they are *your* flowers! In thanks for such a grand tea this afternoon."

She accepted the flowers with a smile, and buried her nose in their exotic perfume. "They are beautiful. Thank you, Lord Wayland."

Elizabeth watched them, a suspiciously smug smile on her face. "Well, then," she said. "Shall we have some sherry before we depart? Or perhaps some tea? We do want to hear of your time in Spain, Lord Wayland. Both my husband and my brother were there, you know . . ."

Chapter Five

Lady Beaton's ball was indeed a "dreadful crush," just as predicted. The line of carriages went around Grosvenor Square, and the receiving line of those guests that had already arrived went through the front doors and down the marble steps.

Georgina did not mind the delay, though. It only meant that she had more time to sit in the warm darkness of the carriage with Lord Wayland, without the distractions of a crowded ballroom.

As Elizabeth had whispered in her ear while they gathered their cloaks, he even liked small dogs and brought flowers *before* a ball.

Lud, was the man *perfect*?

So Georgina set herself now to find a fault with him, as she studied him where he sat across from her. His nose *was* a tad crooked, as if it had once been broken. His cheekbones were rather sharp, and the lines about his eyes were too deep for his youngish age, as if he had been squinting into the Spanish sun too long. He did not possess the smooth olive beauty of so many of her Italian friends. Or the golden perfection of her first husband, Jack.

No, Alex possessed something much more interesting than mere bland beauty. His features spoke of intelligence and experience, of pride.

And there was certainly nothing wrong at all with his figure. His shoulders required absolutely no padding, and his breeches fit his long legs like . . .

Georgina turned away, fanning herself. Very well, then, so there were no faults there. She looked back to him, turning her study to his attire. His cravat was simply tied, with a stickpin of a tiny, insignificant diamond in its snowy folds. His waistcoat was of plain ivory satin. Not very stylish, compared with the pinks of the *ton*. But Georgina, who loved flamboyant fashions for herself, rather disliked it in men. And, having a wide friendship with artistic sorts of people, she had seen some flamboyance!

She much preferred Lord Wayland's quiet elegance.

So, he was handsome, he dressed with good taste, he liked her dog, he had a nice laugh, performed great deeds in the park, was a war hero, *and* a duke.

Georgina conceded with a sigh. He *was* perfect. Probably too perfect for her own flawed self. However, that did not mean she could not enjoy his company while she had the chance.

"I do believe we have arrived at last!" said Elizabeth.

Georgina shifted her attention to the carriage window to see that their wait was indeed over. *Thank the gods,* she thought. She could certainly use a glass of champagne. And had it suddenly become overly warm in the carriage?

A footman opened the carriage door, and Alex stepped out first to assist Georgina and Elizabeth. Georgina was quite touched to see the care he took with Elizabeth; Lizzie thought her condition was still hidden, but it was really becoming quite apparent beneath her lacy sash. It was clear that Alex had apprehended this, and he held her arm tightly to help her ascend the steep front steps.

Georgina left her cloak with the Beatons' footman and joined Alex and Elizabeth at the end of the receiving line, at the foot of the grand staircase. This was always one of her favorite moments of a ball; the chance to look ahead and behind her, and see who was in attendance. To see if there was anyone who might need to have their portrait painted, or if there were any friends to greet.

Tonight, though, there could be no one more fascinating than the person she was with.

Alex detested balls.

They were always overly warm, overly scented with the perfumes of the guests and the masses of flowers, and full of uninteresting conversation. He was also a rather poor dancer, which could often prove quite embarrassing.

He could see, as he and Georgina and Elizabeth at last greeted their hostess and entered the ballroom, that this particular rout would be scarce any different from those he attended since his return to London.

The dancing had not yet begun; the musicians were tuning up behind a bank of potted palms, and the crowd was milling about waiting for the opening pavane. It all seemed very aimless, with ladies exclaiming over one another's gowns, gentlemen inquiring after one another's latest acquisitions at Tattersall's, couples claiming one another for the dances, and footmen moving about with full trays of champagne glasses.

Yet he knew it was not at all aimless. Reputations were made and broken on the whispers behind fans,

the gentleman-to-gentleman asides. It was a precari-
ous, expensive world, one that some people, such as
Alex's brother, would pay anything, do anything, to
stay in. In the end, the gambling and the spending had
broken Damian, and all their family.

And Alex had been far away, unable to stop any of
the madness and unhappiness.

In the midst of these renewed pangs of guilt, he felt
the light pressure of Georgina's fingers on his arm. He
turned to look down at her.

She smiled at him, and went up on tiptoe to murmur
in his ear, "Absolutely horrid, is it not? Like a gather-
ing of clucking chickens."

He laughed. "Horrid."

"Ah, the things we go through for our art, Georgie," Elizabeth sighed. Then she drifted off to greet a
group of friends.

"Indeed," Georgina said. She tugged at his arm.
"Shall we join the fray, Lord Wayland? I do believe
people are beginning to stare."

Alex looked down at her, at her inquisitive green
eyes, and he knew then that he could never be the
cause of another person's unhappiness, as he had been
with his family, being far away and unable to curb
Damian's excesses. He had only known Georgina
Beaumont for a very brief while, but he knew that
she would be very angry, and very hurt, if she found
out about his friends' silly wager, and his own secret
temptations toward her.

He had no wish to see those eyes full of anger. He
wanted them to laugh at him, to sparkle and smile—
to fill with admiration, as he was certain his did now
as they looked at her.

He turned back to the ballroom, and saw that they
were indeed attracting attention. As a new duke, with

a scandal for a brother, he had become accustomed to the attention, even though it still made him most uncomfortable. Yet now he found that a new duke with a beautiful, famous woman on his arm was an even greater object of interest than a duke alone.

Mamas glared at Georgina, even as they urged their daughters to stand up straighter and smooth their hair. Some of the gentlemen, obviously admirers of "La Beaumont," looked crestfallen; others took out their quizzing glasses and eyed the two of them speculatively. Sophisticated young matrons and widows studied Georgina's gown, then looked down at their own lesser creations in chagrined comparison.

The elderly Lady Collins, a notorious eccentric, said, loud enough to be heard even over the large crowd, "Is that that artist chit with young Wayland? I would wager that hair of hers is *dyed!* Never saw that red in nature."

Georgina giggled.

Alex frowned. "What an old harridan that Lady Collins is."

"Nonsense!" Georgina replied. "I plan to be just like her when I am seventy; I will say what I please, and care for none. Is that champagne I see over there? Shall we force our way through the masses and get a glass?"

"What a grand idea, Mrs. Beaumont. I was just thinking the exact same thing myself."

As they ventured into the crowd, Alex looked about for Hildebrand and Freddie. He intended to ask them to call off that silly wager as soon as possible; he did not care two straws if it was "ungentlemanly" to cancel a wager once it was made. He wanted to become friends with Georgina, and he did *not* want such nonsense hanging over them like a dark cloud.

Yet they were nowhere to be found, and he soon found himself in the midst of a large circle of Georgina's acquaintances, all of them eager to be introduced to him. In the middle of their conversation and laughter, he quite forgot about Hildebrand and Freddie and any wagers at all.

"What a handsome fellow your duke is, Georgina!" whispered Lady Lonsdale, a very stylish lady whose portrait Georgina had once painted, and who had become a friend. "I am quite envious."

Georgina laughed, and looked to the dance floor, where Alex was engaged in a country-dance with Elizabeth. "There is no need to be envious, Harriet! He is not 'my' duke. Lord Wayland and I only met this afternoon, and he kindly offered to escort Elizabeth and myself this evening, since Nicholas is from Town."

"Hm. Only out of the kindness of his heart, I am sure." Lady Lonsdale fluttered her feathered fan. "Tell me, how did you and the duke meet?"

"He jumped into the river after my dog."

"Ha!" Lady Lonsdale laughed most heartily. "Are you telling me a corker, Georgina?"

"I assure you I am not! Lady Kate escaped from her lead and went for a swim. Lord Wayland very gallantly rescued her from being carried off, and Elizabeth invited him to take tea with us at her house in thanks."

"Oh, my dear! Such an *on dit*. One of the great heroes of the Peninsula ruining his attire rescuing the dog of a famous artist! It will be in all the papers tomorrow, you know."

"I only hope that the scandalmongers do not imply that I am on the hunt for a new husband."

"Your appearing here with him tonight *will* be sure to cause talk."

"There is always talk. I am quite accustomed to it."

"And you do nothing to discourage it!" Lady Lonsdale's tone was gleeful.

Georgina shrugged blithely. "It is good for my career to be noticed! As long as there is no true scandal. That would be quite disastrous."

The dance had ended, and Alex was leading Elizabeth toward them, the two of them happily laughing and chatting.

"He *is* very handsome," said Lady Lonsdale. "And he does seem to like you a great deal."

"His lordship has been very kind . . ."

"No doubt." Lady Lonsdale lowered her fan, and smiled as Elizabeth and Alex reached them. "Lady Elizabeth! How very radiant you are this evening. Marriage must certainly agree with you."

"It does indeed!" Elizabeth replied merrily.

"When shall we have the pleasure of seeing your scamp of a husband again?"

"Very soon, I am sure, Lady Lonsdale. There was a bit of an emergency at our country estate, which he went to look in on. But may I present his worthy substitute this evening, His Grace the Duke of Wayland? Lord Wayland, this is our friend, the Countess of Lonsdale. Georgina painted her portrait last year, and she is a great patron of art!"

"So you must be certain to be nice to her!" Georgina laughed.

Alex grinned, and bowed to Lady Lonsdale. "I shall endeavor to do my best, Mrs. Beaumont. How do you do, Lady Lonsdale."

"You must not listen to their fustian, Lord Wayland! They will have you believing I am an ogre who does naught but sit for portraits all day, and lord it over poor, groveling artists," said Lady Lonsdale. "I am very glad to meet you, though, Lord Wayland. I have heard that you performed quite a dashing feat in the park today. I am sorry I missed it."

"Yes, well, rescuing fair damsels in distress is a specialty of mine."

"So I understand." Lady Lonsdale smiled at him over her fan.

The orchestra struck up the lilting strains of a waltz, and Alex turned to Georgina. "Mrs. Beaumont, would you do me the great honor of dancing with me?"

"Thank you, yes." As Georgina accepted his arm and went with him to the dance floor he had only just vacated, she said, "I feel I should warn you, though, that I bring more enthusiasm to the dance than grace."

"I will confess in turn—my feet are of the two left variety." One of his hands slid into hers, and the other landed warmly at her waist. "But I daresay we shall rub along well enough together."

"I daresay we shall."

Indeed they did. Their steps seemed well matched, and soon they were swaying and swooping amid the other couples, taking the corners in dashingly executed spins that sent Georgina's emerald green skirts swirling.

She laughed merrily after one especially energetic turn, bringing the gazes of the other dancers in their direction. "I cannot recall when I had such fun waltzing!"

"Nor I! Dancing is usually a bit of a chore, something I had to do with my sister at country assemblies when I was a lad. But this is quite nice. Quite— different."

"So the evening has not proved to be so tedious as you had feared?"

"How did you know I feared it would be tedious?"

Georgina smiled slyly. "I have my ways!"

"Well, I never expected that *your* company would be tedious. And this ball has not been at all, thanks to you and Lady Elizabeth."

Georgina hummed a bit to the music as they turned and swayed. "I do believe this is an Italian song. I could almost think myself home again!" She closed her eyes, and smiled at the blissful moment of music and Alex's warm arms about her.

All too soon, the music ended.

Georgina found herself quite unaccountably disappointed.

"Shall we take a stroll on the terrace?" Alex asked. "It is sure to be cooler outside."

"Oh, yes, what a lovely idea!"

There were several couples gathered on the Beatons' terrace, walking, talking quietly, or watching the brightly lit ballroom through the open doors. A few bolder guests could be glimpsed slipping about the garden beyond.

It was quite an extension of the ball, but much cooler, and lovely beneath the stars.

Georgina leaned against the marble balustrade, and sipped at the glass of champagne she had caught from a footman's tray on the way out of the ballroom. It was truly a beautiful night. The London sky was uncharacteristically clear, lit by an almost full, pale silver moon. The scent of early roses from the garden hung sweet in the air. The champagne was cool and delicious as it slid down her throat.

And Alex's arm was warm and delicious when he leaned on the balustrade beside her.

"Do you miss your home in Italy very much, Mrs. Beaumont?" he asked quietly.

Georgina smiled at him. "Dreadfully."

"Will you tell me about it? I have been to Spain, and France, and Belgium, but never to Italy."

"Are you certain you wish me to speak of it? Once begun, I often cannot stop!"

"I am certain. Tell me, please."

"Well, I have two homes in Italy. One is a small villa at Lake Como, which I purchased after my second husband passed away. It is quite old, sixteenth century, and something is always falling to bits. The plasterer has to be called in almost every year!" Yet even as she complained, her face lit with a small smile.

"Were there no more modern houses available in the area?"

"Oh, yes, certainly. But this particular one boasts a very fine fresco in the room I use as a dining room, a lovely work of a classical party group eating grapes and dancing. There is also a very good view from the terrace, where I often have luncheon parties when the weather is especially fine. And there are endless vistas for sketching!"

She paused to sip at her champagne, and Alex did the same. He turned her words over in his mind; they had conjured for him a vision of not only a beautiful place, but of a life lived beautifully, with friends and parties and endless vistas of loveliness.

He so envied her in that moment.

He drained his glass, and said, "What is your second home?"

"That is my city home, in Venice. A very small place, also very old and crumbling, but not without its own charms! Elizabeth and her husband have purchased a house just across the canal, and they visit me there in the winter."

"I am truly jealous, Mrs. Beaumont."

She laughed brightly. "Jealous, Lord Wayland? Of me? Why, you are a duke! Surely you possess far finer properties than my small homes."

Alex thought wryly of the large town house, and the hunting box in Scotland, both lost to his brother's profligacy. "I think what I am jealous of is your freedom. It is obvious that you love your life, that you love what you do."

Georgina tilted her head, gazing up at him quizzically. "I do. I think there is nothing more wonderful in life than to have a blank canvas before me and a paintbrush in hand, with an Italian scene to paint. And I have the best of friends, who share that passion. But what is there in your own life, Lord Wayland, that you would wish different? What would you wish to put in its stead?"

He looked down at her, standing there beside him in the moonlight. A tiny frown of concern pleated her ivory brow. He wanted, more than anything he had ever wanted before, to kiss her. He wanted to kiss away that frown, to hold her against him, and lose all his troubles in her warmth and happiness.

He even lifted his hand a tiny bit toward her, but he was saved from his own folly by Elizabeth's voice calling to them from the open terrace doors.

"There you two are!" she said. "The last dance is about to begin, and then of course there shall be a mad dash for supper. You would not wish to miss Lady Beaton's lobster patties."

Alex's hand fell back to his side.

Georgina laughed, and placed her empty glass on

the balustrade. "Certainly not! I have heard such glorious things about those lobster patties."

"As have I." Alex held out his arm to her. "Shall we?"

Her hand was as light as a bird on his sleeve. "Thank you, Lord Wayland!"

As they reentered the ballroom, Alex at last caught a glimpse of Hildebrand and Freddie, just as they were departing. They saw him, and sent him laughing little waves before they left, their heads together as they whispered gleefully.

"Was that not your friends? Mr. Marlow and Viscount Garrick?" said Georgina. "Do you not wish to go after them and bid them good evening? I could save you a seat in the dining room."

Alex took one last glance at Hildebrand and Freddie's departing figures, then shook his head. "Anything I have to say to them can certainly wait until tomorrow. The lobster patties, however, cannot wait."

Chapter Six

"Was the ball last night not a crush? I vow all the *ton* must have been there," Elizabeth sighed.

It was very nearly noon, but they were only just beginning their morning toast and chocolate in the breakfast room. All the morning papers were spread across the table, as they perused them for mention of their names and descriptions of various gowns and *on dits*.

"Hm, quite," Georgina replied as she spread marmalade on her toast, almost dragging the ribbons of her morning gown through the stickiness. She was not yet entirely *awake*, though she did notice, with much gratification, that they were mentioned several times in papers. "Even that funny old Lady Collins was there."

"And everyone seemed quite interested in your handsome escort!"

"*Our* escort, Lizzie!" Georgina protested. "Did Lord Wayland not escort both of us to the ball?"

"Well, yes, of course. Most proper. But anyone could see it was *you* he was there for, you he was interested in. How could he not be? Every young buck in Town is at your feet."

"Lord Wayland is hardly a young buck. He is quite the most distinguished gentleman I have met this Season."

"Oh, yes. Quite." Elizabeth grinned mischievously. "Perhaps even the most distinguished gentleman you have seen in—years? I know I have not seen anyone so distinguished."

"Are your husband and brother not so, Lizzie?"

"I love Nick with all my heart, and in my eyes he is the finest man in the world. Yet *distinguished* is not the first word that springs to mind when one thinks of him. Peter, of course, is quite distinguished in his own fashion, and is much less formidable since Carmen and Isabella came into his life." Elizabeth frowned in thought. "But Lord Wayland has an openness and amiability that I fear my dear brother often lacks. His manners were very charming, as I'm sure you must agree, Georgie."

"Yes," Georgina murmured. She stared down into her half-empty cup of chocolate. "Very charming. You are right in saying that it has been a long time since I have met such an amiable man."

"Not since—Jack?" Elizabeth suggested gently.

"Lizzie!" Georgina protested. "Jack has been gone for almost ten years. I have met many men since then. I even married two of them."

"Old men you married out of desperation and pity," Elizabeth argued. "Have you never thought of marrying again for affection or even love?"

Georgina laughed. "My dear friend, it is good of you to try to matchmake for me! But I only met Lord Wayland yesterday, and here you have us wildly in love and off to Gretna Green."

"Not Gretna Green! St. George's, Hanover Square."

"Lizzie . . ."

"Oh, all right! I won't say another word. But, Georgina, I do only want your happiness."

"I *am* happy! I have everything I have ever wanted. I have my work, independence, wonderful friends, and a lovely home. I am quite content."

"All those things are delightful, Georgie, as I well know. My own work is so vital to me. Yet a good marriage can make all those things even more splendid; it can make life complete!"

Georgina shook her head. "*Good* marriages are few and far between. I have ample proof from the horrid things my clients have told me of their husbands, as they sit for portraits."

"I, too, hear dreadful things. Not every marriage, though, is like that. Nick and I are very happy, as are Peter and Carmen. You and Jack . . ."

"Marriages like those are rare. I had my one love. And I will never give up any portion of my delicious freedom for anything less!"

"No," Elizabeth said quietly. "Of course you will not. You *should* not."

"Excellent. Then, may we cease to discuss my matrimonial prospects, and decide what we want to do this afternoon?"

"We must plan my *salon*, of course! It is to be *next* Friday, and I have not begun a thing. But first, will you tell me one thing, Georgie?"

"What is that?" Georgina asked warily.

"Will you at least *see* Lord Wayland again?"

"Oh, yes. In fact, he is calling at four to take me driving in the park."

Elizabeth caught up the folded copy of the *Gazette* and tossed it at Georgina's laughing head. "Horrid

girl! Not to tell me, *me*, your bosom bow, and let me
rattle along like that!"

"Oh, Lizzie!" Georgina giggled. "I am sorry to keep
it to myself. You just looked so very earnest and dear,
arguing for matrimonial bliss."

"Hmph." Elizabeth looked over at Lady Kate, who
was perched in the window seat, waiting for the day's
excitement to begin. "Do you see how shabbily we are
treated, Lady Kate? After all our good attempts to assist!"

"Lizzie! I will cry peace. I will keep you informed
of all my social engagements from now on. Now, I
have something very important I should like your advice on."

"Oh, yes? What is that?"

"What should I wear on this drive?"

Georgina studied the array of garments laid out
across her bed, all of them neat and fashionable muslins and silks in every color of the rainbow. She held
up first one then another in front of her, twisting about
before the mirror.

"What I really need is something new," she mused
as she tossed another rejected gown onto the pile.
"Something stunningly original!"

Except that a *modiste* would take at least a week
to fashion something "stunningly original," and Lord
Wayland would be calling for her in an hour. And
Georgina was already possessed of a wardrobe that
was original, and overly vast to boot.

She flopped down before her dressing table. "Why
am I being as fidgety as a schoolgirl?" she asked Lady
Kate, who was peering out from beneath the hillock
of frocks.

The dog's ears perked up, and she tilted her head
as if considering.

"I am thirty years old," Georgina continued. "This is hardly the first time I have gone driving in the park with a handsome gentleman. And I have never thought twice about what to wear before!"

Lady Kate whined.

"Yes, quite! I suppose Lizzie has a point. There must be something unusual about this Wayland. Something—special."

Lady Kate barked.

"Exactly! Therefore, I must spend more time with him. Either he shall prove himself to be no different from any other charming man of my acquaintance, or he will show what it is that makes him so special."

Lady Kate's tail wagged vigorously.

Georgina knelt down beside the bed to receive a doggie kiss on the nose. "You are the best conversationalist I have ever met, Lady Kate. Most understanding. Best of all, I know you will never tell anyone of my cabbage-headed behavior today! Will you?"

Lady Kate sighed.

"You are not going to wear *that* coat, are you?" Hildebrand said, around a mouthful of Alex's leftover luncheon beefsteak.

Alex look down at his completely respectable, as he had thought, green coat. "What is wrong with it?"

"My dear fellow, what is *not* wrong with it?"

"The color is bilious," offered Freddie.

"The cut all wrong through the shoulders," said Hildebrand.

"And the length . . . !" sighed Freddie.

"Oh, very well!" Alex tore off the offending coat and tossed it onto a chair. "What do you suggest I wear in its place?"

"Where are you going?" asked Hildebrand.

"Not that it is any of your business, pup, but I am going driving in the park."

"Alone?"

"With a lady," Alex growled.

Hildebrand and Freddie glanced at each other speculatively. "Mrs. Beaumont!" they cried.

"My dear fellow," clucked Hildebrand. "You cannot escort such a dashing lady dressed like a country curate. Where are your other coats?"

"There." Alex pointed at an abandoned pile on the carpet.

Hildebrand left his steak and went to poke at the pile with the toe of his boot. "Do you mean to say that you tried on every coat you own, and that that green *thing* was the best you could find?"

Alex's jaw was taut. "Yes," he answered shortly.

Hildebrand clucked in dismay. "Wayland! You must hie to Weston immediately, at once!"

"Hildebrand. Even if I could fly out the door and land at Weston's doorstep, it would not help me this afternoon. I am due to call on Mrs. Beaumont in less than an hour."

"If only he could still wear his regimentals!" Freddie lamented. "Ladies find them demmed attractive."

"If only. It looks as if you've had these shabby bits since before you bought your commission, Wayland!"

"I have. Most of them," Alex said.

Hildebrand shook his head. Then he plucked up the blue coat from the top of the pile. "Wear this one, then. The color at least is good, and it looked fine the other day. Then tomorrow, Freddie and I will take you to the tailors ourselves."

"Yes," said Freddie. "Can't be shabby if you're going to dangle after an heiress."

Alex froze in the act of shrugging into the blue coat, and turned a glare onto the hapless Freddie. "I am not *dangling* after anyone. I am merely going for a drive in the park with a lady."

"Of course, of course," Freddie stammered. "N-no insult meant, Wayland. None at all."

Hildebrand turned Alex toward the door, away from the hapless Freddie. "Well, Wayland, you should be going! You will be late, and ladies do not like us to be late. Do they, Freddie?"

Freddie took a gulp from his wineglass. "Not at all!"

Alex glanced at his watch, and saw that he was indeed about to be late. He gathered up his hat and gloves, and turned one more stern glance onto his friends. "Very well. Just try not to drink *all* my wine while I am gone."

"No! Of course we would not do that."

"Of course." Alex paused at the door. "And one other thing—I want to have a talk with the two of you about that ridiculous wager you concocted."

"Wager? What wager?" Hildebrand cried, all innocence. "You *really* should be going now, Wayland."

"Very well. I will speak with you later, then." Then Alex left, closing the door softly behind him.

Hildebrand and Freddie ran to the window, to grin and wave as Alex's curricle drove away.

"D'ye think he fell for it all?" Freddie asked anxiously.

"Of a certes," said Hildebrand in great satisfaction. "We will be toasting our friend's health at his wedding breakfast before the Season is out!"

* * *

Alex glanced up once to his window before he guided his curricle into the traffic, and saw his friends waving and smiling like a pair of bedlamites.

They were up to something, he could tell. Ever since the three of them had first met at Eton, Freddie and Hildebrand had always behaved like the silliest clunches when they were concocting a scheme. Sometimes it had been smuggling a toad into a don's bed, or coaxing a larger allowance from their fathers, or trying to catch a pretty opera dancer's attention.

Now, it obviously had something to do with him.

But right now, Alex had weightier matters to consider than what those loobies were about. Matters such as Georgina Beaumont. And why he was so very anxious to see her again.

Perhaps it was only that he had been gone from England for so long, and then immured at Fair Oak when he did return. He had been in company with his fellow officers' wives in Spain, of course; and in Seville there had been a lovely innkeeper, Concetta. Yet it had been a long time since he had spent any amount of time with a pretty, unmarried *Englishwoman*.

Yes! he thought in relief. That would account for it. He had simply formed an infatuation for the first lovely woman to smile at him. In the clear light of a respectable afternoon drive, without the excitement of a swim in the river or the glitter of a ball to distract, he would see that really she was quite ordinary. Then there would be no more hours of anxiously thinking about her, of waiting until he could respectably see her again.

And he could get on with more businesslike and unpleasant matters—such as trying to raise some blunt.

Alex drew up his curricle outside Lady Elizabeth's town house and leaped down, much relieved by his thoughts. Now he and Georgina could enjoy their afternoon, without any silly romantical thoughts interfering!

Then he saw her again.

She emerged from the house before he could even ascend the front steps. She was wearing an afternoon dress of sunshine-yellow muslin, with sheer, gauzy white sleeves and a gauze Vandyke collar. It seemed she was *made* of light today; the late afternoon sun reflected on her brilliant hair and the yellow of her gown, and Alex's eyes dazzled as he looked at her.

She put on the bonnet she held, a white straw confection tied with wide yellow ribbons, and then came toward him, her hand outstretched. Her merry smile could have eclipsed even that sun.

Alex knew then, with a desperate, sinking sensation, that the feelings that had struck him when first he saw Georgina had not been mere gratitude for her attention, or his long deprivation of female company.

Those feelings had come from *her*, and her alone. From the sheer force of her beauty and her vibrant personality. She was unique, she was—special.

"Oh, Lord Wayland!" she said, taking his hand in her own gloved one. "How very good of you to rescue me from madness."

Still much struck by these new and strange emotions, Alex assisted Georgina into his curricle and climbed up beside her. He had never been so glad of anything than he was to have the reins and the driving to distract his thoughts. "Madness?" he asked.

"Yes. You see, Lizzie has decided to launch her own *salon*. Every Friday evening she will invite painters, writers, singers, what have you to her drawing room."

"It sounds delightful."

"Oh, yes! No doubt it will be. But she intends to hold the first one next Friday, and this afternoon she is in an uproar trying to decide exactly *who* to invite, and what food to serve." Georgina sighed. "Right now, the butler, the cook, little Isabella, and Lady Kate are all gathered together, offering their opinions, and Elizabeth is nay-saying them all. I tell you, I escaped only just in time. Perhaps, if we are gone a *very* long time, all will be settled by the time I return."

Alex laughed, his heart lightened, his doubts forgotten. As he had the day before, he quite forgot all his worries the moment he was in her company. Money, marriage, his family—there would be more than enough time to worry over those when he was deprived of her presence.

"Then, Mrs. Beaumont, I shall endeavor to take the long way about the park," he answered with a grin. "If there *is* a long way."

"If there is, I am certain we can find it."

"And, when the *salon* does come off, I am sure Lady Elizabeth will have a mad crush on her hands, and invitations will thereafter be highly sought for her Friday evenings."

"Of that I have no doubt. Certain high sticklers do not entirely approve of Lizzie, but she is the very center of a younger, more dashing set here in London. The *salon* will be a great success, and fun as well." She smiled at him. "You will be invited, of course. As will your friends, Mr. Marlow and Viscount Garrick."

"Now, that invitation I happily accept! I cannot speak for my friends, though. They are good enough fellows once you get to know them, but not precisely what one might call artistically minded."

"So I have gathered, from our very brief acquaintance!" Georgina laughed. "But I'm sure they would add an interesting element to the guest list."

"Then I will pass the invitation on to them."

Alex watched Georgina from the corner of his eye as she laughed and turned her face up to the warmth of the sun.

"You really are very lovely," he blurted, before he could even think.

Then he felt his face burn.

Chapter Seven

Georgina looked at Lord Wayland in shock, wondering if perhaps her ears had deceived her. A *compliment*, from the so-perfect duke? And a blush from him besides!

She found herself hopelessly, absurdly delighted. She even had the most unaccountable urge to giggle. Several swains in Italy had composed poems to her "emerald" eyes; some had even written songs and then sung them beneath her window. No flowery tribute had ever moved her so much as the fact that Lord Wayland thought she looked lovely today.

How very curious.

She waited until the need to giggle and simper had passed, then said, "Thank you very much, Lord Wayland! What a very kind thing to say."

He smiled at her, a wide white flash against his sunbronzed skin, and Georgina once again felt the giggles coming upon her.

She covered her mouth with her gloved hand.

"I speak only the truth, Mrs. Beaumont," he answered. "But I am sure that you must hear how lovely you are every day."

"Oh, not *every* day," Georgina answered lightly. "Every other day only, Lord Wayland."

"Then, I shall have to make it every day," he said. "If you will but do one thing for me."

"What might that be?" said Georgina, hoping against hope that it might be a kiss.

"Will you call me Alexander? Or Alex. Lord Wayland makes me feel too fusty! It makes me look about for my father."

Georgina smiled. Well, it was not a kiss, but it was a very nice thing nonetheless. "Very well. Alex suits you so much better than Lord Wayland. And you must call me Georgina."

He smiled in return. "Done."

As they turned into Hyde Park and joined the parade of worthies, Georgina thought that Alex seemed more at ease than he had when he first arrived at Elizabeth's house. When she had emerged to greet him, she had had the very odd sensation that he had not quite been expecting *her* to be there; as if he had arrived to escort someone else and had gotten her by mistake. He had looked quite surprised.

In the midst of all her excited anticipation, she had felt a small prick of uneasiness. She liked him so very much, had so carefully prepared for their drive. What if *he* did not like *her* so much? What if all the easy accord she had sensed the night before had been all in her imagination? What if she was making a wigeon of herself over a man who could have no regard for her?

The confident, sophisticated artist existed only in front of the scared, lonely, awkward orphan she had once been. At the thought of looking foolish in front of this man, little Georgie Cheswood completely took over Mrs. Georgina Beaumont.

But not now. Now Alex seemed more the man who had fished Lady Kate out of the river, who had waltzed so *vigorously* with Georgina. He was smiling, at ease, seemingly happy as he nodded to the people they drove past.

So Georgina, too, relaxed, and set herself to enjoying the sunny afternoon and the lovely man beside her.

"Your horses are very grand," she said.

"Scylla and Charybdis. They are not perfectly matched, I fear," Alex answered ruefully. They were, in fact, a pair that had once belonged to his brother, and were now almost all that remained of the Kenton stable. "Not at all fashionable."

Georgina examined them, one perfectly chestnut and one with a white star on its brow and white socks. They *were* prime goers, even if not perfectly matched. "Perhaps not. But they are strong and healthy, and very graceful. Good-looking, too." Much like their master, she reflected. "I should love to have some like them for my own curricle."

Alex looked at her, one brow raised in surprise. "You own a curricle, Mrs. Be—Georgina?"

"Oh, yes. It is not here, of course. It is at my villa. When I want to drive here, Elizabeth's husband gives me the loan of his."

"Yes," he said slowly. "I did hear that you and Lord Pynchon were to have a race."

Georgina laughed. "So you have heard of that! Yes. That silly popinjay was spouting off about how women should never drive, because we are so slow and such menaces on the road. So I asked if he cared to make a small wager on that point."

"Did you?" Alex's voice was quiet. "Do you often gamble, Georgina?"

Georgina remembered then, much to her mortification, that Alex's brother, the late Duke of Wayland, had caused a great scandal with his huge gambling losses. Even in the *ton*, who often routinely lost hundreds of pounds on the turn of a card, he had been notorious.

"Oh, no," she hastened to assure him. "A bit at silver loo now and then, but never high stakes. And I hardly ever wager. Only to bring ridiculous loobies like Pynchon down a peg. I have much better things to do with my money."

"Such as that charming bonnet," Alex murmured. "Well, if you ever need to go driving, my horses are at your disposal."

"Why, thank you, Alex!" Georgina cried. "They *are* darlings. And you must be sure to come and watch me trounce Pynchon. It will be an easy victory over one so ham-handed! Everyone will be there."

"When is the race to be?"

"A fortnight from Saturday, at the White Hart Inn, just outside of Town."

"I shall be sure to be there."

"Excellent! Oh, look, there is Lady Lonsdale waving to us. Shall we go speak to her?"

"By all means." But as Alex turned toward where Lady Lonsdale waited, perched on her gray mare, he looked at Georgina with a rather serious gleam in his eyes. "You will be very careful in this race, will you not, Georgina? And you will have a physician in attendance?"

"How very solemn you are!" Georgina laughed lightly, but she was secretly pleased that he was so very concerned. No man had been careful of her or her well-being for such a very long time. "Of course I will be careful. And you will be there to watch out for me, will you not?"

"Oh, yes," he said. "I will certainly be there."

*   *   *

"I had a very nice time," Georgina said, accepting Alex's hand as he assisted her from the curricle. "I never would have thought I could say that about a sedate drive through the park at the crowded hour, but so it was!"

Alex's hand lingered on her own for one long, warm, sweet moment. Then he stepped away. "I, too, enjoyed the afternoon."

"Will you not come inside to say hello to Elizabeth?" Georgina stepped around to pat Scylla's and Charybdis's noses in farewell.

"I fear I have kept you quite late, and you will be wanting to prepare for your evening."

"Oh, we are having a quiet evening at home. Elizabeth was rather tired from her exertions at the ball last night, and I insisted she rest."

"Yes." Alex hesitated, then said, "Forgive my boldness, Georgina, but is your friend quite well?"

"Well? She is, er, in a delicate way."

Alex blushed just a bit, which Georgina again found so charming. "I *had* perceived that! But I mean, is she having a difficult time of it? She seemed pale last night, and a trifle short of breath."

Georgina frowned. "I confess I have been rather concerned. She tries to pretend that everything is the same as ever it was, but it is not. She is so tired, where before she never was."

"My old nursemaid, who is now retired to a cottage on my family's estate, saw my mother very ably through four difficult confinements, and only one of the babes was lost. She has a great knowledge of herbs and cures. If you like, I could give you her direction and you could write to her. I am certain she would love to share her knowledge with you."

Georgina felt the prickle of incipient tears. She blinked very hard, and turned to bend her head over Scylla's neck. Never had she been so touched by a man's thoughtfulness. How many men of her acquaintance would be so concerned over the health of a strange woman and that of her unborn child? Concerned enough even to speak of the indelicate.

None would be. None but this man.

"That is so kind of you, Alex," she said softly. "So *very* kind! Elizabeth is my dearest friend, really almost my sister. I will do everything I can to help her."

"Yes. Of course. Well." Alex coughed, and shifted his feet uncomfortably.

Georgina almost smiled at that adorable discomfiture.

"Perhaps," he continued, "if Lady Elizabeth is feeling well tomorrow, you and she, and Lady Kate and Lady Isabella, would care to take a picnic to the country? I am sure my friends Marlow and Garrick would accompany us. Fresh air and sunshine would probably be beneficial to Lady Elizabeth."

"I am sure it would!" Georgina cried. "That would be most pleasant. I will speak with Elizabeth, but I know we have no fixed engagements tomorrow."

"Then, we shall call for you at noon." Alex took her hand, and raised it to his lips. "Until then, Georgina."

"Yes. Good day, Alex."

Georgina watched him until his curricle turned a corner, out of her sight. Only then did she go inside the house, her hand curled carefully around that kiss.

"Georgie!" Elizabeth called through the open drawing room door. "Is that you?"

"Yes, it is me." Georgina left her gloves and bonnet on a table in the foyer, and went into the drawing room.

Elizabeth was ensconced on a chaise before the fire, a blanket tucked about her and a book open on her lap. Dark purple smudges still shadowed her gray eyes, but she seemed a trifle less pale.

"How are you feeling, dear?" Georgina sat down next to Lady Kate in a deep armchair across from Elizabeth.

"Oh, much more the thing! I had some tea and biscuits earlier, after I settled some points about my *salon*, and Lady Kate and I have been having a coze. I even think I might enjoy a bit of trout for supper!"

"Lizzie. I know I have said it before, but I must say it again. You should go to the country, to Evanstone Park, and rest."

"Georgina!" Elizabeth laughed. "Don't fuss so, dear. If I do feel worse, I will go to Evanstone and wait for the baby to make its appearance. For now, though, I am quite well. I want to stay here in Town, and enjoy myself with you and our friends, just for a bit longer."

"If you are quite sure . . ." Georgina said uncertainly.

"I am sure! Now, enough about me. I want to hear all about your afternoon with the handsome Lord Wayland."

Georgina settled back in her chair with a blissful sigh, the golden afternoon still warm around her. "It was delightful! Lord Wayland is such a fine man, so very kind. He was all that is amiable. He even offered to let me drive his cattle, which are quite fine." Georgina paused, stroking Lady Kate's soft fur thoughtfully. "I do think, Lizzie, that perhaps Lord Wayland—or Alex, as he asked me to call him—is not *all* that he shows to the world."

Elizabeth looked up, surprised. "Whatever do you mean, Georgie? Not all that he shows?"

"Oh, I do not mean that he hides dire vices behind a pretty facade! Far from it. I suppose I should have said he is *more*," Georgina mused.

"Well, I would not wonder at it!" said Elizabeth. "His family must be quite in a stew still."

"How do you mean? What do you know about the Kentons, Lizzie?"

"Only gossip, really. If I knew anything ill of Lord Wayland, I would have told you straight away. But Nick knew Damian Kenton, Alex's brother, slightly, during his old raking days before our marriage."

"The late duke? I have heard so many rumors about him. What was he really like?"

Georgina and Elizabeth leaned their heads together in avid interest.

"A bad 'un," whispered Elizabeth. "Always gambling, whoring; he lost huge amounts, without a thought for his family."

"Hm, yes. Alex said something about his brother's gambling."

"Yes. But this present duke, I think, is not much like his brother," Elizabeth suggested. "Would you not say so, Georgie?"

Georgina smiled. "Oh, yes. I would definitely say so."

"Then, you will see him again?"

"He has asked us all—you, me, Lady Kate, and Isabella—on a picnic tomorrow. Do you think you feel well enough?"

"Of course! The fresh air will do wonders for me, and the baby. I quite look forward to it!"

"Good. So do I."

                    *   *   *

Georgina lay awake long into the night, turning Elizabeth's words about Alex's family over in her mind.

So Damian Kenton had been a wastrel, just as she suspected. Racketing about Town, losing money, while his mother and sister sat in the country, and his younger brother fought for his country in Spain and at Waterloo.

Perhaps that, then, was a part of the secret solemnity in Alex's so-blue eyes. Perhaps he felt guilt that his family had been in such straits when he was too far away to help them. Helpless to shield them from his brother's excesses.

How well Georgina knew that feeling! Helpless guilt had been her companion throughout her childhood.

She rolled onto her side, to watch the bar of moonlight that fell from her window across the carpet. There was also one other, small thought that bothered her.

If Damian Kenton had been such a terrible spendthrift, what was the condition of the Kenton fortunes now?

Not that she cared a great deal for such things. She had lived in genteel poverty for much of her early life, and she knew very well that honesty and humor were to be valued above gold. Money was merely something that—facilitated life.

But now she was wealthy. She could sense that Alex was a proud man, and if he was in dire straits, he could find the idea of a friendship with her to be made awkward by vulgar lucre. Or, even worse, he could find friendship with her sweetened by her money.

And Georgina would not care for that at all!

Chapter Eight

"Georgie, do you think these flowers look better here, or over on that table?"

Georgina tilted her head, examining the large vase of pink and white roses. "They look lovely in either place."

Elizabeth sighed in exasperation. "That is not very much help! The guests will be arriving in an hour, or less, and I cannot even situate the decorations. At least the refreshments are prepared and laid out." She glanced toward the open doors of the dining room, where a sumptuous repast was spread. "Perhaps the crab cakes would have been better than the mushroom tarts?"

"The mushroom tarts are delicious!" Georgina paused before a mirror, and straightened the amber combs in her hair. She smoothed the bodice of her saffron-gold gown. Was it just a trifle *too* low-cut? Would Alex like it?

She giggled, and tugged the satin bodice just a bit lower.

"Georgina, you are not attending!" Elizabeth cried.

"Of course I am," Georgina answered. "Why are

you so very worried? You have given many routs before, Lizzie."

"This is my first *salon*, and I want it to be a great success. I want people clamoring for invitations to my Friday evenings!" Elizabeth picked up the vase and moved it to the other table. "Here, I think."

"It was so very charming over there, though," a masculine voice drawled.

Elizabeth whirled around in a flurry of sapphire silk skirts. "Nicholas!" she cried, and ran across the room to fling herself into her husband's arms. "You are here at last! I thought surely you would never arrive in time."

Nicholas kissed her, and held her close against him. "I'm sorry, my love. We had a broken wheel on the road. But I swore to you I would not miss your *salon*, and here I am." He smiled at Georgina. "Hullo, Georgie! You are stunning, as always."

"Thank you, Nick. I am very glad you are here; you can persuade your wife to cease rushing about and sit down, before her ankles swell."

"My ankles are *not* swollen!" Elizabeth protested. But she did sit down, and propped her slippered feet up on an embroidered footstool. "How did you find Evanstone Park, my love? Not too much damaged, I hope."

"Nothing that couldn't be repaired. The storm did a nasty job on the roof over the east wing, though." Nicholas poured himself a measure of brandy from the array laid out for the party, and sat down next to his wife. "What have you two been up to while I've been away?"

"Nothing out of the ordinary way," said Elizabeth. "We went on a delightful picnic yesterday, and attended the Beaton ball last week. A terrible crush, as always."

"I hope that you have been resting enough, Lizzie," Nicholas said sternly.

"Of course I have!" Then Elizabeth grinned mischievously. "And Georgina has a new admirer."

"Another one?" Nicholas laughed. "Georgie, you really ought to leave *someone* for the other ladies."

"I hardly have *every* man in London at my feet!" Georgina protested.

"Oh. Only half, then?" asked Nicholas.

"No! And he is not my *admirer*, Lizzie."

"Of course not. He is just here every day, escorting you to balls, and on picnics and drives. Sending flowers . . ."

"He is being kind. He has been away from England for so long; he doesn't know anyone else yet."

"That is not it at all, and you know it!" said Elizabeth. "He obviously likes you. He probably wants to marry you."

"No!" said Georgina firmly. "I am hardly suitable."

"You are the most suitable! He could do no better. I think that he . . ."

"Ladies, please!" Nicholas interrupted. "Who is this new admirer that has the two most unflappable women I know in such an uproar?"

"Alexander Kenton," said Georgina. "The new Duke of Wayland."

Nicholas's dark brows shot up. "Hotspur Kenton?"

"You know him?" Georgina asked hopefully.

"I knew *of* him, in Spain. Everyone knew of Colonel Kenton of the Sixteenth. He was absolutely fearless, but an excellent leader; never asked his men to do anything he wouldn't do himself. I had heard that

Damian had finally stuck his spoon in the wall." He grinned at Georgina. "So he is your new suitor, Georgie? Should I have a talk with him, find out his intentions?"

Before Georgina could respond to this bit of nonsense, the knocker at the front door sounded, and Elizabeth jumped out of her chair.

"The guests are arriving!" she cried. "Does everything look quite all right?"

"Perfect, darling," said Nicholas. "Now, I will go upstairs and change my clothes before I disgrace you." He paused to kiss Georgina's cheek. "See you later, Duchess."

Georgina smacked him on the shoulder.

The *salon* was proving to be a rousing success.

Painters, poets, musicians, patrons of the arts, and even politicians stood in groups large and small across the drawing room. They spilled out onto the small terrace, and flowed into the dining room where the refreshments beckoned. The mushroom tarts were consumed; the champagne was drunk; the harp and the pianoforte were played. Elizabeth was glowing with pleasure at her success, and the two paintings of Georgina's that were displayed were greatly admired.

In short, it was looking to be a rather perfect evening, aside from one small flaw.

Well, a rather large flaw, actually. Alex had not yet appeared.

Every time the drawing room opened to admit a new flood of guests, Georgina would turn eagerly, searching their faces, only to be disappointed.

What was wrong with her, behaving like a silly schoolgirl when she was all of thirty years of age? Men handsomer than Alex Kenton had taken her driving before, had escorted her to balls and routs. They had been charming, pleasant company, enjoyable to flirt and dance with. And she had forgotten them almost as soon as they were out of her sight.

Why should this man be any different?

Because, she admitted to herself with a rueful sigh, he *was* different! She had so wanted him to see her paintings, to see how admired they were, that she had a talent. That she was not a mere empty-headed Society matron, dabbling in watercolors.

Because she wanted him to admire her, blast it! To be intrigued by her.

As she admired him. And was intrigued by him.

But how could she win his admiration if he was not even here!

". . . do so love this one, Mrs. Beaumont!"

Georgina turned her attention from the door to smile at the woman beside her, a small, blonde viscountess who had been examining her paintings. Georgina could not, unfortunately, remember which viscountess she was.

"Oh, yes?" she said helpfully.

"Yes!" The viscountess gestured with her glass of champagne at an informal study Georgina had done of Elizabeth, Nicholas, Lady Kate, Isabella, and Elizabeth's brother and sister-in-law, Peter and Carmen, the Earl and Countess of Clifton. They were gathered around a tea table on a country house terrace, a scene of domestic harmony and great friendship, much laughter and love.

Georgina smiled to recall that particular golden afternoon at Evanstone Park, when she had been sketching away to capture the scene.

"I would vow I was there!" the viscountess—was it Lady Dalrymple?—continued. "You have captured the scene so beautifully. Is it perhaps available for purchase, Mrs. Beaumont?"

Georgina shook her head. "I fear not. That was done only for my own pleasure. As was that one." She indicated her other work on display. It had the setting of the same terrace, but it was a solitary portrait of Carmen. A tall, raven-haired, striking Spanish woman, she was posed dramatically against the white marble of the terrace in a mantilla and gown of black lace.

Georgina had resisted all the efforts of Carmen's husband to buy it from her. There was something about it that reminded Georgina so poignantly of her days following the drum on the Peninsula with Jack.

"An excellent likeness of Lady Clifton," Lady Dalrymple said. "Such a pity neither of these works are available! Perhaps, however, you will be in London long enough to begin a new work? I had been thinking of a new portrait of myself, to present to Lord Dalrymple on our anniversary."

Georgina smiled, sensing a new commission. "Perhaps, Lady Dalrymple, you would permit me to call on you some time next week, so we may discuss it further?"

"I would be ever so delighted, Mrs. Beaumont! Now, I must go and speak with Lady Elizabeth. Her *salon* has been such a quiz!"

Georgina watched her leave, then turned back to her own painting. It truly was a scene of great marital harmony; Nicholas standing behind Elizabeth, his hand on her shoulder as he looked down at her open sketchbook. Little Isabella cuddled on her father's lap, while her mother leaned forward to tie her little slipper ribbon. Lady Kate dozed contentedly in a patch of sunlight.

A perfect instant, captured forever.

Georgina loved it, this scene of her dearest friends. It cheered her immensely; yet it also made her feel rather wistful. Lonely, even.

"It is truly exquisite," a man said from behind her.

Georgina looked over her shoulder, and gave a small cry of delight. "Alex! You have come."

"Yes. I do apologize for my lateness." He moved up beside her, peering closely at the painting with his quizzing glass. "I am just an old army man, of course, and know little about art. But I can truly say that that is one of the loveliest paintings I have ever seen."

Georgina had received many compliments on her work over the years, many of them from more knowledgeable critics than this one. None, though, had ever made her feel like crying with utter joy.

Just as his compliments on her beauty had made her feel like giggling and blushing.

"I thank you," she said. "This is my favorite painting I have ever done; it brings me great happiness."

He nodded. "A scene of great beauty. I can see why it would make you happy just to look at it." He looked down at her, and smiled. "Though I do wonder, Georgina, why you looked so sad as you examined it a moment ago. Was there a flaw that you just detected?"

Georgina's gaze flew up to his. "I did not—how did you . . . ?"

"Oh, I have a rather embarrassing confession to make," he said with a rueful little laugh. "When I first came in, I stood over there and watched you in secret for a moment."

Georgina looked away, flustered. And very pleased. "Alex, how silly! Why would you do that?"

"Because you looked so very pretty," he said softly.

Then his jaw tightened. "That was a very clumsy compliment. Forgive me."

"What is there to forgive? First you admire my painting, then you say I look pretty. Such calumny!" she teased.

He smiled, and turned rather awkwardly to the portrait of Carmen. "Is this your only other work displayed?"

Georgina nodded, letting him change the subject. "Yes. Do you know the Countess of Clifton?"

"I have met her once or twice. She was of invaluable service to us during the war."

"She is a very fascinating person, and a joy to paint. I think she has passed on her beauty to Isabella!"

"So she has. But I am rather surprised, and disappointed, not to see more of your work."

"Oh, Elizabeth would have covered the walls with my paintings if I had let her. I did not want to appear *ostentatious*, though."

Alex threw back his head and laughed extravagantly, a deep, warm sound that caused heads to turn in their direction. "Georgina," he said, "I fear you cannot help but be a bit ostentatious! Your beauty will always make you conspicuous."

"A-ha!" she cried. "Another compliment. That is three in one evening."

"I seem to be quite the poet tonight."

"So you are. Well, Lord Byron, if you would truly like to see more of my work, and are not just being polite, I would be happy to show it to you. I am sharing Elizabeth's studio while I am here, and I have several pieces in there."

Alex glanced around uncertainly.

"You needn't worry about my reputation," she said. "I am no young miss you will be forced to wed if you're found alone with me! I am only going to show you my paintings; it's all quite respectable, and we will not be gone long."

He grinned. "You will think me quite old and fusty."

"Not at all! But maybe *you* should be wary of your reputation, being seen with a lady rogue like me." She caught up some glasses of champagne from a footman's tray. "We will just take these with us."

The studio, faced on two sides with windows and with a skylight overhead, was flooded with moonlight. Silvery shadows were cast around props and easels; satin drapes seemed to undulate from the corners. It all seemed terribly romantic, a perfect spot for secret trysts and whispered, passionate words.

Georgina forced such fanciful thoughts from her head, since it was obvious that Alex had no such intentions on this night. She lit a lamp that sat on a small table, and set about taking holland covers down from her finished paintings.

"These are mine," she said.

Alex stepped closer to examine them. They were mostly portraits, of course; two of a duchess and a baroness that were waiting to be sent to their subjects, and one of Isabella. There was a wedding portrait of Elizabeth and Nicholas, and several small studies of Lady Kate.

He spent the longest time on the last three works. He even drew out his quizzing glass to look at them, turning his head this way and that.

Georgina could hardly stand it. She hated it so when people looked at her work and did not say anything; she always imagined the worst, that they disliked it.

"What do you think?" she asked at last.

"Beautiful," he breathed. "You are truly gifted, Georgina. Even I can see that."

She laughed in profound relief. "Did you think I was just some fluffy-headed female, dabbling about with watercolors?"

"Certainly not! No one ever *buys* fluffy watercolors. But to see them—thank you, Georgina, for giving me this privilege."

"I am the one who is privileged, to share what I love so much with someone who appreciates it. Which do you like the best?"

"Well, your portraits are certainly fine. You have quite captured your subjects, both their outward appearance and their personalities. Why, I can almost *see* the mischief in Isabella's eyes!"

"Yes! It was quite a struggle to make her sit still for longer than two minutes."

"They are lovely. These, though—I feel I am *there*, in all three of them."

Georgina examined the paintings under discussion. "Landscape is rather new to me. I have always sketched the places I have been, but I never tried it on a larger scale until recently."

He gently touched the painting hanging in the middle. "This is your villa in Italy?"

It was a sun-drenched scene of a white stucco villa, crowned with red tiles and iced with wrought-iron balconies. In the distance could be seen the azure expanse of Lake Como.

"Yes," said Georgina, "that is Santa Cecilia."

"And the others?"

"This one was painted in Scotland when we were there on holiday last year." She indicated the vision of a ruined castle, set atop a hill covered with purple heather. Then she turned to the last, a small, cramped, dark-stained house, set back in a tangled garden, with a storm breaking over it. "This is the house I grew up in."

Alex looked from the painting to Georgina, his blue eyes serious. "Not a very cheerful aspect."

"No. Never go to gloomy Sussex, if you can help it!" Georgina forced a light laugh, and turned away from the painting. She went to sit down on the chaise she used for her models, and poured herself a glass of champagne.

"Is Sussex so gloomy?" Alex leaned back against the wall, watching her.

"Perhaps not so very, all of the time. Perhaps just the home of the Reverend and Mrs. Smythe."

"Your parents?"

She shook her head fiercely. "Never! My aunt and her husband. I painted that when I went back there a few years ago, for my aunt's funeral." She held up the glass. "Care for some champagne?"

"Yes, thank you." He came and sat beside her, taking the glass she handed him. "Would you tell me about them? About your childhood?"

"It is very dull."

"I don't care," he answered, surprisingly intent. "I find I want to know everything about you, Georgina Beaumont."

Georgina studied him carefully, longing to see the truth of those words in his eyes. Longing to trust this man, this perfect man, with the truth of her less than exalted past.

Then she nodded.

"My parents, Gerald and Maria Cheswood, were carried off by a fever when I was just ten years old," she began. "My father was the youngest son of a baronet. His family disowned him when he married my mother, the daughter of a merchant from Bristol. They refused to take me in when my parents died, so I had to go to my mother's sister, my Aunt Hortense, and her husband, the Reverend Smythe."

"They of the gloomy house."

"Yes. It was not very much like living in my parents' home! My mother was a very *joyful* woman, and so affectionate. She was always devising games and parties, so we were very merry, even though there was not much money. And she and my father were very much in love." Georgina paused to take a deep sip of the champagne. "In the vicarage there was no joy, no affection. Only sermons and housework. Endless housework. They deeply disapproved of me, you see; disapproved of my red hair, and the fact that I laugh at things that are funny."

"It sounds dismal," Alex said quietly.

"So it was! It certainly showed me what I did *not* want my life to be like. But then, when I was fourteen, a miracle happened."

"What was it?"

"My aunt decided it would be best if I was sent away to school."

"School was a miracle?"

"To me it was. You see, three things happened to me there. Mrs. Bennett, who taught art, was the first. I had always scribbled, you see, but she taught me technique, color. She made me see what a wonder art could be, what a salvation."

"The art world owes a great thanks to Mrs. Bennett, then!" he exclaimed. "What were the other things?"

"When I was sixteen, Elizabeth came to the school. She also loved art, and we became bosom bows. As we remain to this day."

"And the other?"

Georgina looked down into her glass, deep into the golden bubbles. "When I was almost eighteen, the brother of a schoolfriend came to visit her before his regiment went to the Peninsula. His family did not approve of me, just as my father's did not approve of my mother, but Captain Jack Reid and I went to Gretna Green a month after we met, and then I followed him to Portugal." She looked up at Alex. "He was killed almost two years later."

"I am sorry, Georgina. So many good men were lost there."

"Yes."

They were quiet for several minutes, wrapped in moonlight and champagne and thoughts of times past.

"I have bored you quite enough, I think!" Georgina said at last, with a laugh. "I want to hear about *your* childhood now."

"Oh, no!" Alex shook his head. "That *is* a dull tale."

"I want to know everything about you," she said, echoing his earlier words to her.

"Then you shall. Another time."

"Yes," Georgina sighed. "We have been gone rather a long time, and I did promise you there would be no scandal."

Alex took her hand and raised it to his lips. "Thank you for sharing your paintings with me, Georgina. And for talking with me."

Georgina stared at their joined hands, expecting to see sparks shooting from them, or perhaps even moonbeams, so delicious were the feelings that emanated from his skin on hers. Alas, that heat was all in her mind; there was only her pale fingers in his sunbronzed ones.

She wished, with all her being, that they could just sit that way, together, forever.

Chapter Nine

By Jove, but he had wanted to kiss her!

Alone in his quiet lodgings, Alex ruminated on the evening, on missed opportunities.

She had been so very lovely, the lamplight turning her hair to pure flame, her green eyes wide as she looked up at him. Her hand had been soft in his, and she had smelled so very tempting with her rose perfume. He had never been so tempted by anything in all his life. Had never wanted to do anything more than he had wanted to kiss Georgina Beaumont.

She had wanted to kiss him, as well. She had leaned gently toward him as they talked; had watched him carefully, quizzically. She was no green girl; surely she had sensed his own desire.

Probably she was wondering now what had made him run away so cravenly.

Just as he was wondering himself.

Alex threw himself back into his armchair with a deep groan. The truth had to be acknowledged now, if only to himself.

He did want Georgina Beaumont, in the physical sense. He found her beautiful, and desirable beyond belief. But he also wanted much more from her than her body. Her confidences in the quiet studio had proven that beyond a doubt.

He was so proud, and pleased, and moved that she would tell him of herself, of the woman behind her glittering Society self. He wanted to know more, to know *everything*. To know about her marriages, her friendships, her home, her favorite food, her favorite color.

More than that, *he* wanted to confide in *her*. To tell her of his troubles, ask for her advice. Relate all his happy childhood memories, his life in the army, his hopes for the future. He had always been a great one for keeping his own counsel, for there had never been anyone he felt he *could* talk to. Now he found himself wanting to tell all to this woman.

This woman he had known only a few days, but who it felt as if he had known forever.

Alex sighed, and closed his eyes. Yes, the veriest truth was that he was no hardened rake like his brother had been. He could not take Georgina as his mistress, no matter how great his desire for her was. He wanted her for his wife, his duchess, his love.

So, a small voice said at the back of his mind. *You ask her to marry you, you have a wife you adore, and plenty of money besides. Where is the rub?*

Ah, he answered that voice, as a wise man once wrote, therein lies the rub. Money.

If he asked Georgina to marry him, he would have to tell her all. That his brother had squandered his family's fortune, and they were left with little more than Alex's army pension. That they would need some of her money to rebuild.

She would surely laugh him out of her life, being

the independent spirit that she was! She thought well enough of him now, when she thought him a distinguished, self-possessed, self-made man. What would she think of him then?

Truly, he had never had a luckier, or more disastrous, moment than when Lady Kate decided to take a swim in the river.

He would just have to take things slowly with Georgina, and bide his time until he could see his way clear to what he should do.

"It was a lovely *salon*, was it not?" Elizabeth said happily, wriggling her stockinged toes where they lay on her husband's lap, being rubbed.

Georgina lolled on the chaise, warm with champagne and happy memories of those moments in the studio. "Umm, lovely. A great success."

"Yes. So many people came there was scarce room to move. And even more will come to the next Friday evening, I am certain."

"Is a *salon* not a chance for great conversation, my love?" Nicholas asked with a teasing grin. "One can hardly have a fascinating conversation if one cannot even breathe."

"There was a great deal of conversation!" Elizabeth protested. "Was there not, Georgie?"

"Hm? Oh, yes. Certainly."

"But I noticed that *you* quite vanished, for nearly an hour," said Elizabeth. "You minx."

"Yes!" Georgina cried merrily. "I do freely admit to minxdom. I was showing Alex my paintings in the studio."

"Oh-ho!" said Nicholas, waggling his eyebrows comically. "Alex is it now?"

"He *asked* me to call him Alex."

"What happened in the studio, Georgie?" Elizabeth asked in desperately curious tones.

"Nothing happened," answered Georgina. "At least not in *that* way. We talked."

"Talked? For all that time? What about?"

"Lizzie!" Georgina protested, laughing. "Such curiosity. We only talked of this and that. Nothing of consequence. I find him very pleasant company."

"Pleasant company, eh?" said Nicholas. "Well. Nothing wrong with that, is there, Lizzie my love?"

"Of course not," Elizabeth answered slowly. "I find him to be quite a pleasant gentleman myself. Does that mean that nothing of a more—serious nature is happening, Georgie?"

Georgina took the last sip from her champagne, then looked down into the empty glass, puzzled by Elizabeth's question. How could she answer something that she herself did not know? "I—well, honestly, my dears, I am not sure. Perhaps there is. He is not the sort of man one can just flirt lightly with, is he? I do like him, very much. I am not sure, however, what his feelings are toward me."

Elizabeth and Nicholas stared at her in obvious shock.

"Oh, my," Elizabeth said finally in a small voice. "Well, of course he must be in love with you. Almost every man you meet is in love with you! He is very fortunate to have your affection in return."

"People would say *I* am the fortunate one," Georgina answered. "To have the interest of a duke. If indeed I do have his interest, which I am not at all sure of."

"Are you saying you are feeling—uncertain, Georgie?" Elizabeth said, her eyes growing even wider. "You?"

"Yes, me! I am—oh, I just don't know. I do not know what my feelings are for him, or his for me, or what is happening at all." Georgina placed her empty glass carefully on a small side table and stood. "I do, however, know one thing. I am tired, and I am going to retire now."

"Would you like to drive my curricle tomorrow? Get in form for your race with Pynchon?" said Nicholas. "We could all go into the countryside for the morning, and have luncheon at the White Hart Inn."

"That sounds delightful." Georgina kissed his cheek, and Elizabeth's. "Good night, my dears. It was a lovely evening."

"Good night, Georgina," they echoed.

"And please do not talk about me as soon as I leave the room."

"Would we do that?" cried Elizabeth, all wounded innocence.

"I am only warning you."

Georgina left the drawing room and closed the door behind her. But she left it open a tiny crack, and leaned her ear against it.

"Do you think she is in love with him?" Elizabeth asked.

"Oh, yes," Nicholas answered. "Undoubtedly. Have you ever seen Georgie *flustered* about a man before?"

Elizabeth sighed happily. "Hm. Yes, I do believe that you are right. It must be love."

Georgina smiled, closed the door all the way, and went up to find her bed.

Chapter Ten

"Pardon me, my lady, but there is a gentleman caller," announced Greene, Elizabeth's butler.

Elizabeth, left alone for the morning while Nicholas and Georgina went driving, looked up from her sketchbook in surprise. "A gentleman caller? Why, here I had thought my days of attracting suitors were long over!" She pressed her hand to the small bulge of her stomach with a laugh.

Greene sniffed in disapproval. "It is Lord Wayland, my lady. I told him it was not your at-home hour, but he insisted."

"Lord Wayland?" Elizabeth interrupted. "Surely he has asked for Mrs. Beaumont, not me!"

"He did first inquire after Mrs. Beaumont, but when I informed him she was on an outing, he asked if you were at home."

"Oh, yes, Greene! Do show him in."

As the butler departed, Elizabeth struggled to her feet, and glanced around the morning room in great consternation. Things were in such disarray, with her own sketches and some of Georgina's piled about everywhere. Shawls and hats were tossed around, Nicholas's newspapers were trampled on the floor, and Lady Kate sat before the fire busily gnawing on a bone she had unearthed in the garden.

Elizabeth took it away from her, much to Lady Kate's consternation, and shoved it under a shawl.

"Hush, Lady Kate!" she admonished. "It would never do for a duke to think we are slovenly."

Lady Kate sat back on her haunches with a loud huff, but she quickly cheered up when Alex came in the room. She bounded up to him, barking in joy.

Alex bent to pat her head. "Good morning, Lady Kate." Then he straightened, with a smart bow for Elizabeth. "And good morning to you, Lady Elizabeth. I trust I find you well?"

"Quite well. I fear, though, that Georgina is not at home."

"Yes, your butler said she was on an outing."

"She and Nicholas and my maid Daisy have gone to the countryside, so Georgina may practice her driving before the race next week. I was meant to go with them, but mornings are not—er, not my best time." She laughed nervously.

"No," he answered kindly. "I should imagine not."

"I am joining them for luncheon. Perhaps you would care to come with us?"

"I would, very much. Thank you."

Elizabeth beamed at him. "Well. Would you like to sit?"

Alex looked about at the piles of paper that covered every seat. "I would, but . . ."

"Oh! I do apologize." Elizabeth pushed some sketches off of a chair and waved him to be seated, then returned to her chaise. "I fear we are rather informal in our family rooms."

"Please, don't apologize. I think this is a charming

room." He picked up one of the sketches, a scene of a country pond. "Is this one of G—Mrs. Beaumont's?"

"Oh, yes. Lovely, is it not? And you needn't call her anything but Georgina in front of me. I won't tell."

Alex laughed ruefully. "You will think me foolish, Lady Elizabeth! Mooning over sketches and such."

"Never! A man who has the good sense to admire Georgina could never be a fool. Except for this man named Ottavio, whom we knew in Venice. He took to serenading her every night beneath her window. Quite gave the neighbors fits, as he sounded rather like a dying cow . . ." Elizabeth broke off. "But I don't wish to bore you with my ramblings!"

"On the contrary. I am all fascination." He placed the sketch carefully on a table, then sat back in his chair. "You have known Georgina a long time, I understand, Lady Elizabeth."

"Oh, yes. Since we were at school. Georgina was a bit older than me, but we quickly bonded over our mutual love of art. She is my dearest friend."

"Then, I should very much like your counsel. If I may?"

"Please do!" Elizabeth leaned toward him in interest. "There is nothing I love more than to give advice."

"I would like to know if—that is . . ." Alex looked away, a faint, warm blush spreading across his cheekbones. "Do you think Georgina would ever want to marry again?"

"Well," Elizabeth breathed. "Are you planning to make her an offer?"

"I—might be." He shook his head. "Lady Elizabeth, I must be completely honest with you. I think your friend is the most fascinating person I have ever met. I want more than I have ever wanted anything to make her my wife, to do anything in my power to make her happy. Only you can tell me if I have any hope."

"Only Georgina can answer that for certain," Elizabeth said carefully. "I do know that she admires you. I also know that her marital history has not been— entirely satisfactory."

"She told me of her first husband. Captain Reid."

"Yes. Jack was very dashing, and Georgina was devastated when he died. She did not tell you of her other two husbands, though?"

"No. There was not time."

"They were no Jack Reid!" Elizabeth's voice dropped confidingly. "In their seventies, the both of them. She married Sir Everett out of desperation. She had only enough money to return to England when Jack died, and only his meager widow's pension to live on. Her family, and his, refused to take her in. So when Sir Everett met her and made her an offer, she could see no choice. He wanted a housekeeper, you see, but was too much a nip-farthing to pay for one. He was a terrible bully; Georgina's letters to me then were quite despairing. Fortunately, he died after only a year, and left her a tidy portion."

"Dreadful," said Alex. "Was the next one as bad?"

"No. Mr. Beaumont was quite an old dear, and so besieged by his grasping children. Perhaps you are acquainted with Mr. Theodore Beaumont, who is so fond of pink waistcoats?"

Alex grimaced.

"Exactly so. Well, Mr. Beaumont had been a friend of Sir Everett's, and he and Georgina had become friends as well. By the time old Sir Everett died, Mr. Beaumont was quite ill. So he asked Georgina to marry him, and help keep his children at bay. So she did, and hired herself an art teacher. She had always been so talented, you see, and in the year she lived on Mr. Beaumont's estate, she developed that talent into what you see now."

"How did it end?"

"Mr. Beaumont died, of course. Peacefully, thanks to Georgina. He left all that was not entailed to her, which so infuriated his children. Georgina's portion amounted to over fifty thousand pounds, you see."

"Good gad," Alex gasped. "Fifty thousand?"

"Yes."

"I—never would have thought it so much." Alex's healthy color drained away, leaving him pale as the white damask of his chair. "She would never have me."

"Why not?"

"A woman of such fortune?" He laughed, a humorless bark. "Of course she would not."

"Most people would say that a woman of her background, despite her fortune *and* a flourishing career, would never be equal to a duke."

"I am not most people."

"No. You are not," said Elizabeth. "You have been honest with me, Lord Wayland, so now I will be honest with you. I know that your family's fortunes are not what they once were, due to the regrettable actions of your late brother."

Alex nodded gravely. "I fear that is too true, Lady Elizabeth."

"I also know that Georgina cares nothing for such things. For her, money is only a convenience, and if she lost it all tomorrow she would not care one whit. She would simply find a way to make some more. If she loves you, money, or lack of it, will never stand in her way." She smiled at him. "And I know that you do not care for her because of her fortune."

"I would love her if she were an orange seller," Alex declared.

"Of course! So marry her, if you can get her. I will dance at your wedding with greater joy than I have ever danced before."

"Thank you, Lady Elizabeth. I promise you that I will do my very best to, er, get her."

"I am sure you shall. I give you a warning, though."

"A warning?"

"Yes. Georgina is the dearest, most generous soul. But she has the pride, and the temper, of a lioness. Never cross her, and your courtship is sure to go smoothly."

She almost laughed aloud at the worried look on his face. "A—temper."

"It's the red hair, you know." Elizabeth rose, drawing her shawl about her shoulders. "Now, I have enjoyed our coze, but we should be going, or we shall never be in time for luncheon! I am quite famished."

"There's Elizabeth now!" Georgina drew up the curricle in the yard of the White Hart, and waved as Elizabeth leaned from one of the inn's windows. "Are we very late, Lizzie?"

"Not at all! We were early."

"We?" called Nicholas, alighting from the curricle and reaching up to assist Georgina.

"Lord Wayland came with me, isn't that grand? We shall be such a merry party!" Elizabeth waved again, then withdrew, pulling the casement closed.

"Why, Georgie!" Nicholas teased. "Are you blushing?"

"Certainly not!" Georgina protested. She did, however, feel just a trifle warm.

"You *are* blushing! Looks terrible with your hair."

"How insufferable you are, Nick!" she laughed. "However can Elizabeth tolerate being married to you?"

"It's because I'm so handsome, of course." He held out his arm. "Shall we go in? Your wild driving has given me quite an appetite."

"That 'wild driving' is going to win me fifty pounds of that dreadful Lord Pynchon's money, come Thursday. I will confess to being a bit peckish myself, though." Her steps quickened a bit as they entered the inn.

"And eager to see Lord Wayland, too, what?"

"Of course not! Ah, here we are."

A substantial luncheon was already laid out in the White Hart's best private parlor, cold meats and cheeses, vegetables, and a lemon trifle.

Elizabeth was busily dipping pickled onions into heavy cream and plopping them into her mouth, while Alex watched her in appalled fascination.

"Hello, my dears!" she cried, wiping cream from her chin. "How was your drive?"

"Marvelous! Nick's new curricle is a wonder; I must order one for myself." Georgina kissed Elizabeth's cheek, then sat down next to Alex, drawing off her gloves. "You are feeling better, I see, Lizzie."

"Yes! Quite well again. And Lord Wayland here has been quite an amusing escort on the drive out."

Georgina smiled at Alex. "It was good of you to come, Alex. Such a grand addition to our luncheon party!"

"How could I resist the company of two such charming ladies?" said Alex, pouring Georgina a glass of wine. "And you, too, Hollingsworth. We did not have much chance for conversation Friday evening, and I had heard that you, too, were an army man."

Nicholas grinned. "Who has been spreading rumors about me? Yes, I was in the army, in Spain. Before I met Lizzie and settled to being a responsible family man."

"Ha!" said his wife, popping another onion into her mouth.

"I was told you were wounded at Alvaro," said Alex.

Nicholas's expression grew quite somber, and he reached for the wine. "Yes, I was. So were Lizzie's brother and his wife. A sad day for our family."

"A sad day for many," Alex agreed quietly. "I did hear that General Morecambe . . ."

"Gentlemen, please!" Georgina interrupted. "It is too lovely a day to spend in gloomy reminiscences. You will have Elizabeth and me in tears soon, and that will never do. I become quite red and blotchy when I cry. Save it for your club, please."

Alex laughed apologetically, and lifted Georgina's hand to his lips in a quick salute. "You are quite right, of course! We shall discuss whatever you and Lady Elizabeth choose."

Georgina beamed at him.

Nicholas scowled in mock despair. "We all know what *that* discussion will be—art."

"There is nothing wrong with art," said Elizabeth.

"Nothing at all," agreed Georgina. "Are you going to eat *all* those onions, Lizzie dear?"

Elizabeth prodded at the empty bowl with her fork. "I fear I already have. Do you think the innkeeper will bring some more?"

"I daresay he will," Georgina answered. "*I* shall not

be riding in the carriage back to London with you, though!" She reached over to spear a piece of roast chicken. "Speaking of art, did you see that egregious landscape Mrs. Sayers had displayed at her Venetian breakfast?"

"No, I didn't!" Elizabeth replied avidly. "She has been telling everyone that she has a Canaletto."

"Lizzie, if this was a Canaletto, I will eat my new pastel crayons! The light was not at all right . . ."

Nicholas and Alex exchanged subtle, despairing glances over their wineglasses.

Nicholas leaned closer and murmured to Alex under his breath as the ladies grew louder and more excited. "You see what I put up with every day, Wayland?"

"I do see," answered Alex.

"And you may wish to take this on for yourself?"

Alex studied Georgina's animated face, her glowing green eyes, the graceful flutter of her gesturing hands. "I think I very well might. How do you find it, being married to an artist?"

Nicholas grinned. "My dear chap," he said, "it is bloody *marvelous*."

"Your friends are very—animated," Alex said as they strolled along a country path after luncheon.

Georgina smiled. "Yes, they are. Quite out of the common way."

"That must be why you are such great friends."

"Hm?"

"You are rather out of the common way yourself."

Georgina studied him carefully, searching his expression for any kind of censure. She did not see any there, only open, honest humor. "Is that a compliment?"

"A very great one, I assure you."

"Then thank you. *You* are rather out of the common way yourself." She sat down on a fallen log, tucking the skirts of her Pomona-green carriage dress about her. "Elizabeth and Nicholas are the only people I feel I can truly be myself around. And now you, of course."

He sat down next to her, at a proper distance but close enough that she could feel the warmth from his shoulder and thigh.

She longed to rest her head against that shoulder. But she feared he would think her fast, even more so than he might already, so she simply folded her hands in her lap instead.

"Do you mean that, Georgina?" he said quietly, almost eagerly. "That you feel able to be yourself with me?"

"Yes. You are not at all what I always suppose dukes to be like."

"Oh? What do you suppose?"

"That dukes are stuffy, toplofty creatures with too much starch in their cravats. Or that they are arrogant lechers!"

Alex laughed. "I am not like that, then?"

"Not at all. You are one of the least toplofty people I have ever met. And not at all arrogant or a lecher!"

"Well, I was not brought up to be a duke. I was brought up for the army, just as if had I had a younger brother, he would have been brought up for the Church."

Georgina picked up a leaf that had fallen onto her skirt, and twirled it around idly. "Tell me, Alex, did you like being in the army?"

"Very much. I was never terribly comfortable in Society, and my parents were very social people, always trotting my brother and me, and later my baby

sister, out for their suppers and card parties. It was a
relief to escape that, to be among men who valued
discipline and camaraderie above witticisms and a fine
leg for dancing."

Georgina grinned at him. "And no ladies expecting
you to do the pretty?"

Alex laughed. "There *were* ladies about, to be sure,
but they were soldiers' wives, and accustomed to a
less exacting society." He paused for a moment, then
went on thoughtfully, "I did not like it all, of course.
Battle is such a hellish thing, and the times between
could be deadly dull. But in many ways it was a life
that suited me, like trying to uphold a peerage could
not. I do miss it."

Georgina feared she knew of what he spoke. She
would hate it if she were forced to give up the art she
loved for a more narrow, constricted existence.

Such as that of being a duchess, for example.

She shrugged off these misgivings, and said, "Well,
I think you will make a superb duke. From all ac-
counts, a far better one than your brother!" Then she
startled guiltily. "Oh! How very rude of me, to say
things like that about your family. Sometimes I do
speak without thinking."

Alex laughed. "Georgina, what you said is far
milder than what I have said myself about Damian!
And what I have heard my mother say." He shook
his head. "I daresay I may be a better duke than poor
Damian was. As much as I dislike it."

"Alex, I . . ." Georgina broke off, not certain what
it was she had wanted to say.

"There is one thing that I appreciate about being a
duke, and giving up my commission."

"Oh? What is that?"

"Coming back to England and meeting you, of course."

She smiled at him, and gave in at last to the temptation to rest her head on his strong shoulder. He smelled wonderful, of wool and starch and soap, and of Alex. "That is something I, too, appreciate."

They sat together quietly for a while, warm in the sun, listening to the birds and the distant voices from the inn yard.

And Georgina knew that there was one other thing she greatly appreciated, a gift that Alex had given her that she had so lacked in life. Had so craved.

Stillness.

But finally the sun slipped below the tops of the trees, and Georgina bestirred herself to rise. "We should be going, I suppose. We are meant to attend Lady Carteret's musicale this evening."

Alex rose beside her, and took her hand in his as they turned their steps back toward the inn. "I suppose your friends will be looking for us."

Georgina, thrilled to her very soul at the feel of her hand in his, said in a daze, "I doubt it. Lizzie is probably napping, which she does every afternoon now. She and Nick can go home in the barouche, if you will ride with me in the curricle."

"I should be delighted."

"Good! I do need to practice my driving a bit more."

"Georgina." Alex tugged on her hand, halting their steps. "Are you certain you wish to drive in this race?"

"Of course! I made the wager. I can hardly decamp now."

"Will it not be very dangerous?"

Georgina looked up at him quizzically, at his frown and the hard set of his jaw. "Why, Alex. Are you *worried* about me?"

"Yes, by Jove, I am!" he cried.

"That is so very dear of you, to worry. I assure you, though, I am an experienced driver. Even though I can be a bit reckless at times, I am not stupid. If something feels not right on the day of the race, I will not drive."

"I know you are not stupid. Far, far from it. It is only . . ." His hand tightened on hers. "If anything were to happen to you, Georgina, when I have only just found you, I think I should run mad."

Chapter Eleven

The day of the race was bright and clear and warm, perfect for the crowds of *ton*nish people who flocked to the old post road in carriages and on horseback. Many had brought picnics, and one enterprising soul was even selling lemonade and sugared almonds.

Lady Kate, on her lead and safely ensconced in the open carriage with Elizabeth and Nicholas, ran from side to side, barking at all the excitement and looking frantically for her mistress.

Georgina, already settled into Nicholas's curricle at the starting point of the race, tried to remain oblivious to all the noise and commotion. She absently smoothed the skirt of her new sapphire blue carriage dress, focusing on the road ahead.

She pretended not to see Lord Pynchon, his balding dome of a head glinting in the sunlight, as he smirked at her from his own equipage. She had greeted him politely when she had first arrived, and she had seen the fear in his eyes, hidden beneath the arrogance.

Alex stood next to her left side, tall and handsome, one hand resting near her knee.

She tried to ignore him, as well. It would never do

to be distracted by the way his hair curled back from his forehead while she was trying to stay on the road!

"I wish you had let me loan you Scylla and Charybdis," he muttered, glaring at Lord Pynchon. "They are the steadiest goers."

Georgina smiled without taking her eyes from the road. "I know they are, Alex, and I vow I would have loved to drive them! But you would not want to cause an *on dit* by loaning me your cattle."

"Do you think people would say I had wicked intentions toward you if you were seen with my horses?"

"Do you have wicked intentions?"

He leered up at her comically. "Of course! Don't *you* have them toward *me*?"

Georgina laughed. "Naughty man! You are trying to distract me. Now, go over and sit with Elizabeth and Nicholas, please."

"Very well." His hand touched hers briefly, warmly, hidden in the folds of her dress. "Georgina," he said solemnly. "Do be very careful."

"Yes. I will. Then we shall all have a lovely champagne supper after, to celebrate my great victory!"

Alex went to the Hollingsworths' carriage, and stepped up to take his seat beside Lady Kate. She clambered up onto his lap, kissing his chin joyously, and he held her paw and waved it in Georgina's direction.

She waved back, then gathered up her reins as Alex's friend Freddie Marlow stepped up to the mark. He fired off the starting shot, and Georgina burst away down the road, neck and neck with Lord Pynchon.

The shouts of the crowd rang in her ears as she urged the horses to ever greater speed. "Come on, my beauties!" she shouted. "You can do it, I know you can!"

The exhilaration of speed sang in her veins, and all she could see was the finishing line just ahead. It was close, so close, and she was so far ahead of Lord Pynchon . . .

Then there was a tremendous jolt off to her right side, a jarring thud as the curricle tilted precariously.

Georgina felt herself falling, an inexorable slide from the curricle's seat. She fell faster and faster, reaching out to grasp something, *anything*, but finding only air beneath her hand.

She landed then, a hard fall on her back. Vaguely, as if from a great distance and through a thick fog, she heard shouts. A dog barking. A woman screaming—Elizabeth screaming.

Alex's face swam into view above her, pale and drawn.

"Georgina!" he cried. "Can you hear me? Are you well?"

"I—believe I am well," she gasped. Indeed, she felt only numb. Shocked. How could it have ended this way?

"Let me help you to rise." He slid one arm gently beneath her, drawing her up.

Georgina screamed at the sharp pain in her shoulder. Then everything faded to darkness, and she felt no more.

The doctor had at last arrived to see Georgina. Alex, from where he lurked in the darkened corridor outside her room, had only a glimpse of her flame-colored hair against a white sheet before the door shut again. Only Elizabeth was allowed in the room with Georgina; Nicholas and several concerned spectators to the ill-fated race were gathered in the White Hart's common room, drinking and waiting.

Alex had refused to leave his place outside that door.

He sat down on the straight-backed chair that had been placed there for him, and buried his face in his hands.

No matter how tightly he shut his eyes, though, he could not blot out the sight of Georgina, so white and still in his arms. Her scream had been horrifying before she fainted, and her arm, before he had bound it up with his waistcoat, had lain at a sharp angle.

Alex had faced battle many times, had had horses shot from beneath him, had seen death at the end of a French bayonet. He had never been so terrified in all his life as he had been to see Georgina's curricle smash, and her lying so still on the ground.

If she was lost to him, after only just finding her . . .

The door to her room opened, interrupting his dark thoughts, and Elizabeth emerged. Her face was reddened from crying, but she seemed composed.

"How is she?" Alex asked her desperately.

"Alex!" cried Elizabeth. "I did not see you. Have you been here in the dark all this time?"

"'Tis of no matter. Tell me what the doctor said."

"He said she will be well. She has a dislocated shoulder, and her arm is bruised. We will have to wait for her to wake to be sure her head is right, but he thinks there is no cause for worry."

"Her arm—her painting," Alex said, his tongue seemingly unable to form complete sentences.

"She will make a full recovery. She must only be careful for a few weeks, which will surely make her wild! Georgina is never happy but when she has a paintbrush in hand."

Alex laughed in utter relief and joy. Georgina would recover! She was not lost.

"Will you not come downstairs with me now?" Elizabeth said gently. "You should have something to eat, or at least some wine."

"No, I want to wait here. Georgina may have need of me."

Elizabeth took his arm, firmly urging him toward the stairs. "She is in good hands now, and she has taken some laudanum. You will be of no use to her when she is awake and *does* need you, if you are ill. Now, come with me. We will have some supper."

Alex went with her reluctantly. "Are you certain *you* are well, Lady Elizabeth? You look rather tired."

"I am, a bit. It has been a very long day, but the babe is quiet now. Earlier she was kicking and rolling fiercely."

"She?"

"Oh, yes. I am sure it must be a girl, and there is only one name for her, with all her energy. Georgina."

"Indeed." Alex smiled. "I would have thought the world full with only one."

"Georgina," a soft voice called. "Georgie dear, can you hear me?"

Georgina's eyelids felt weighted, as if by lead. She could not open them, or even talk through a mouth gone sticky. She opened her hand, and ran her fingers along the soft linen sheet beneath her.

A bed? When had someone brought her home? And what of the race? Had she lost? What had happened?

Then she remembered. The accident; falling from the curricle. Alex coming to her, lifting her. The awful pain from her shoulder.

She slowly lifted her heavy hand to touch that shoulder. She found the gauzy feel of bandages there, holding her immobile.

"She moved!" cried the voice. "I believe she is awake. Georgina?"

Georgina forced her eyes to open, to focus on the woman who sat beside her. "Lizzie?"

"You *are* awake!" Elizabeth said. "Praise be. I was so worried."

"W-water?" Georgina managed to croak.

"Oh, yes, of course!" Elizabeth held a goblet to Georgina's lips, holding her head as she drank thirstily.

Sated, Georgina fell back against the pile of pillows. "How long have I been—asleep?"

"Several hours, dear."

Georgina turned her head toward the one small window, and saw that it was night. Only the lamp beside the bed gave any light. "Hours?"

"Yes. The wheel of the curricle caught in a rut, and you were thrown from it. Remember? You dislocated your shoulder, and the doctor set it while you were unconscious. He gave you some laudanum for the pain. Are you in any pain?"

"Not at all. I am only so very tired."

"Then you must go back to sleep! We will leave you."

"We?"

Elizabeth gestured toward the doorway, and only then did Georgina see the two men hovering there in the shadows. Nicholas and Alex both looked distinctly worse for wear, their hair on end as if they had run their hands through it, their clothes rumpled.

Georgina smiled weakly. "You two look dreadful,"

she said. "A dislocated shoulder hardly calls for a deathbed vigil!"

Nicholas laughed, while Alex shuffled his feet ruefully.

"We did not know if your head was to rights," Elizabeth explained. "You looked so very pale, and your breathing was quite shallow."

"Well, I am fine now. Where are we?"

"The White Hart. And we shall *stay* here until you are completely recovered."

"I will be completely well by morning, I am sure. But you should be in bed, Lizzie. This cannot be good for the baby." Georgina looked to Nicholas. "Take your wife away now, Nick, and make her rest, so that I can get some sleep."

"Happily, Georgie." Nicholas came to help Elizabeth to her feet, and kissed Georgina's cheek gently. "You gave us such a fright today."

"I apologize, my dears. I promise I shall never do it again. Now, good night!"

"I shall look in on you later," Elizabeth warned.

As they left the room, Alex came to take their place, sitting down in Elizabeth's empty chair.

Georgina reached for him with her good hand, and he took it between both of his. His lips were warm as he lowered them to her palm.

"I was so scared, Georgina," he whispered. "When you fainted away in my arms . . ."

"You, Alex? Who led charges into vast regiments of murderous Frenchies? Scared by a woman's faint?"

"Yes," he answered simply.

Despite the sleepy haze she was in, Georgina wanted to cry. She wanted to cry, and laugh, and shout her thanks to God for sending her this dear man.

But she was far too weak to do any such thing. Instead, she just squeezed his hand. "You take such care of me, Alex. I do not deserve you."

"You deserve much better than me."

"Oh, no, my dear. You are a good, kind, brave soul. I am wild and scatty. Everyone says so, and today you had the proof."

"You are far braver than I," he answered. "Fearless, in a way I never have been."

"Alex . . ."

"This is not time for declarations. You are ill. But you must know, Georgina, how greatly I admire you."

"As I admire you. Of course this is a time for declarations!"

Alex pressed one finger against her lips, stilling her words. "I did not want to press you so soon, Georgina. But your accident has shown me that there is not time to waste in this life. Perhaps, when you are recovered, you would consent to go with me to Fair Oak, and meet my mother and sister."

Georgina was almost shocked speechless. No one had ever invited her to meet his *mother* before. That was for sweet young virgins, for intendeds, for brides.

Oh, great heaven. Alex wanted to *marry* her. To make her a respectable woman, a duchess.

Whatever could she do?

"You—you want me to meet your family?" she stammered.

"Yes. There are things, many things, you should know before you commit yourself to—to anything," he said slowly. "Fair Oak is my home, the best place for you to make any decisions. So will you come?"

Georgina's mind raced furiously. Alex's mother was no doubt quite a high stickler, being a dowager duchess. Would Georgina's manners be acceptable to her? Would her clothes? Her past? Her art?

Whatever would she pack to visit a ducal estate? She would have to visit a *modiste*.

"Georgina?" he said, breaking into her dazed and scattered musings. "Will you? Please?"

"Oh, yes," Georgina replied. "I would be honored to meet your family."

Then she swallowed hard, past the knot of trepidation in her throat.

Despite her exhaustion, and the pain that was once again creeping up on her, Georgina lay awake long after Alex left her. Things were moving so very quickly now, her head spun from it. It was as if the moment of her accident, the second that she had thought her life to be over, had changed everything, had propelled them forward.

Alex's intentions *were* honorable. He wanted her to see his home, meet his family. Be very certain before she "committed" herself to anything.

She had thought that perhaps, just perhaps, he had had serious intentions. Maybe she had even hoped it, deep down in her heart. She had known she would never consent to be his, or anyone's, mistress, so if that had been his wish she would have had to break off all contact with him.

She had intended to never marry again, of course. She so loved her life, her work, her independence. She had thought she would never again meet a man who could respect all that—until Alex.

Georgina had watched him on the night of Elizabeth's *salon*, as he looked at her paintings. He had looked at them with appreciation and respect, had listened to her as she spoke of her work. He was never condescending or dismissive, as so many of her so-called "admirers" were.

Alex was a very special man indeed.

Georgina did have some misgivings over his words that there were "things she should know." But surely there was no harm in just *meeting* his family, seeing his home? If his family disapproved of her, or if she felt uncomfortable with them, it would be better to know.

There could be no harm in this. None at all. Surely.

Reassured, Georgina slid down beneath her nest of blankets, and gave in to her sleepiness, warm, comforted, and full of delicious anticipation.

Chapter Twelve

"Are you quite certain you are recovered enough for this journey?" Elizabeth asked worriedly, as she sat on Georgina's bed and watched Georgina and Daisy sorting through gowns and hats. "Does your shoulder not still pain you?"

Georgina laughed. "You make it sound as if I am going to the pyramids of Egypt! It is only a fortnight in the country, and I promise I will not go riding or driving." She held up a lavender-striped muslin gown, with a low, square neckline trimmed in silver lace. "This is not too daring, is it?"

Elizabeth shook her head. "Perfectly respectable. But, Georgie, I still feel this is too sudden. It has only been nine days since your accident. You still need to rest. Could you not put off this trip until next month?"

"If I did that, it would have to wait until after the exhibition at the Royal Academy. Then Alex will have to supervise something or other at his farm, hay I believe, and guests would be a nuisance. And then it will be time for me to go home to Italy." She held up a white straw bonnet trimmed with yellow feathers and streamers. "What about this?"

"Lovely. It will go with your yellow walking dress. But I still think . . ."

"Lizzie." Georgina placed the bonnet back in its box, and went to sit beside Elizabeth. "Is there something you are not telling me? Do you have some sort of—misgivings about Alex?"

"No! I like him. He seems a very good sort of man."

"Yes. I think so, too."

"We had such a nice talk before your race, and I am sure he thinks very highly of you. As he ought!"

"Then, where is the difficulty?"

"It is not a great one, by any means. It is only—well, you know that his brother was very careless, and frittered away a great part of his family's fortune."

Georgina's hands felt suddenly cold. She tucked them into her lap, and somehow managed to ask, "Are you saying, Lizzie, that you think Alex is after my money?"

"No!" Elizabeth cried. "No. You and I have met many men over the years, and have seen many of our friends' romances flourish or wither. I think we could tell when a man is sincere, unless he is a very good actor. Which Lord Wayland is not! I think he is fond of *you*, not your money."

Georgina nodded. "I believe that, as well." Did she not?

"But he did seem quite shocked when I told him of the extent of your legacy from Mr. Beaumont."

"Alex is—a very proud man," Georgina said slowly, thinking aloud.

"Yes. Prouder even than Nick, I fear."

"It would be difficult for him to feel beholden in any way, even though I would never see it that way. I would—if we were married, I would see it as an equal sharing."

"Then, you must make *him* see it that way, as well! There is nothing else for it, if you truly want him."

"Oh, yes. I believe I do." Georgina bit her lip. "It will not be easy."

"No. Not at all."

"Nothing ever worth having was easily come by."

"How true." Elizabeth smiled, obviously recalling her own rocky courtship. "How *very* true. You must promise me one thing, though, Georgie."

"What is that?"

"Well, my determined friend, that when you become a duchess, in the grandest ceremony ever seen in England, *I* shall give the wedding breakfast."

"Shall we see Fair Oak soon?" Georgina asked, straining for a glimpse of whatever might be down the lane.

They were riding in Alex's curricle, with the baggage coach, accompanied by Elizabeth's maid Daisy, behind, since Georgina had declared that traveling in closed carriages made her feel ill. She was very glad of this, too, for the country they had traveled through was exquisite, a rich, verdant green, and their journey had been most pleasant. They had chatted of many things, and had been completely at ease in each other's company.

Lady Kate, too, was at ease, sitting between them, barking at birds overhead and the occasional fox in the hedgerows.

Now, however, they had turned down the winding, tree-lined lane that led to Fair Oak itself, and Georgina was overcome with an uncharacteristic nervousness. She straightened the small net veil of her fashionable hat, and smoothed the skirt of her new lilac carriage dress.

"Georgina!" Alex said. "Never say you are nervous."

"Not at all!" Georgina protested. "Well—perhaps just a bit."

"My mother and sister will not eat you," he laughed. "In fact, I would be willing to wager that they are far more anxious about meeting you than you are about meeting them."

"Surely not! Why would a dowager duchess and her daughter be anxious about meeting a mere missus, an artist?"

"For exactly that reason. You are quite famous, you know. Mother and Emily have lived quietly in the country for many years. Their only news comes from the neighbors who travel into Town, and from less than respectable newspapers, which Mother has a guilty pleasure in. When I wrote to her that you were coming, she wrote back full of excitement."

Georgina was flustered, and oddly pleased. "She did?"

"Oh, yes. She has heard of you, you see, has read of your art and your gowns, and who knows what. She fears Fair Oak will not be grand enough for you."

"What nonsense!"

"I assure you, 'tis true." They turned a corner of the lane, and Alex pointed ahead with his carriage whip. "There is the house now."

Georgina looked to where he pointed, and gasped. Fair Oak might be too much of an architectural mish-mash to be truly *grand*, but it was very impressive. It towered above the drive and the small park, dark and imposing, looking down on the world through mullioned Tudor windows. Stone gargoyles kept watch from the corners of the roof.

It was a bit neglected, to be sure, just as Georgina

had feared. Ivy crept willy-nilly over the half-timbered walls, which in turn needed a fresh coat of paint. The stone front steps were cracked, and the fountain at the center of the drive was dry.

But these were things easily fixed, and the house itself was lovely. It seemed to give off an aura of the many, many years of family life lived within its walls, of all the love, laughter, quarrels, births, marriages, and deaths it had seen.

It seemed to welcome her.

As the carriage drew to a halt, the front door opened and a young woman stepped out. She could only be Alex's sister, for she had a look of him about her oval face, her straight nose, and her blue eyes. Her golden curls were drawn back and tied with a blue ribbon, that matched her rather faded muslin dress.

She smiled at them, clapping her hands in delight when they descended from the carriage and came to greet her.

"Alex, you are home at last!" she cried, throwing her arms about his neck. "Mother has been asking for you every moment since breakfast."

"You are looking well, Em!" he said, lifting her off of her feet until she squealed.

"I *am* well, now that you are come! And this must be Mrs. Beaumont. I know her from the sketches in the newspapers." Emily stepped back from her brother, and held out her hand to Georgina. "How do you do, Mrs. Beaumont."

"How do you do, Lady Emily. I am so happy to meet you at last, after hearing so much about you."

"Not as happy as we are to meet you! And is this your sweet doggie? I will have the maid take her directly to your room. But how ill-mannered I am being, keeping you out here on the doorstep! Mother has sent for some tea, and she is so eager to meet you." She leaned forward and whispered, "She has changed her gown quite five times this morning."

Georgina laughed, feeling much better about the four times she herself had changed. "Then I will be sure to compliment her on it."

The interior of Fair Oak was much the same as its exterior. The foyer was very grand, crowned by a sweeping staircase and a dome fresco of Grecian nymphs and cupids cavorting against a blue sky. The floor was a lovely, intricate parquet. But there was no rug, no paintings (though there were darker squares on the blue silk wallpaper where some had once hung), and the only furniture was a rather battered mahogany table. The table was itself bare of all ornament except a lovely arrangement of early roses and wildflowers.

"Mother is waiting in the morning room. I hope that you do not mind that we don't receive you in the grand drawing room," said Emily, hurrying across the vast foyer to open one of the many closed doors. "The morning room is warmer, and so much *cozier!*"

"Certainly I do not mind," answered Georgina. "I do so much prefer cozy to grand any day."

Emily gave her a relieved smile. "Wonderful!" Then she turned and called, "Mother! Here are Alex and Mrs. Beaumont at last."

Alex held out his arm to Georgina, and she accepted it, looking up at him through her veil. He had been quiet since they entered the house, and Georgina had sensed him watching her closely, gauging her reaction to his home.

Or at least she hoped it was her reaction he was judging, and not her behavior.

She leaned closer, and whispered, "Your house is beautiful."

"Thank you," he whispered back. "You do not think it too vast, or old-fashioned? Or too—empty?"

"It is certainly vast." Georgina glanced around the furniture-less foyer again. "And perhaps a bit empty. But it has such a welcoming warmth to it. I quite like it."

He smiled then, and laid his free hand over hers. "I have often felt the same about Fair Oak."

"Alexander!" a voice called. "You are not going to keep our guest standing about out there all day, are you?"

"No, Mother." Alex led Georgina into the morning room. "Of course not."

"Yes, I thought I had raised you with better manners. The army, though, might have obliterated them. Come closer, now, so that I can see you."

Georgina's hand tightened on Alex's arm as they approached the woman seated by the fire. She felt a small frisson of nerves, an unaccustomed unease.

The Dowager Duchess of Wayland had the look of her children about her. Her hair was a dark gold, somewhere between the light brown of Alex and the guinea gold of Emily, caught up in soft curls beneath a lacy gray cap. She had the same nose and decided jaw, and the hand she held out for her son to kiss was long, slim, and pale.

The eyes that looked up at Georgina were the same piercing, brilliant blue.

"Are you going to introduce me to our lovely guest?" she said.

"Mother," Alex said. "May I present Mrs. Georgina Beaumont? Mrs. Beaumont, my mother, Dorothy, Dowager Duchess of Wayland."

Georgina gave the elegant curtsy she had been perfecting before her mirror. "How do you do, Your Grace."

Dorothy laughed merrily. "Oh, please, none of that nonsense in my own home! No calling me Your Grace, if you please. Do be seated, Mrs. Beaumont." She glanced at her son and daughter, who were hovering beside her chair. "The two of you sit down, as well. You have both grown so tall, that I cannot talk to you without getting a pain in my neck."

Georgina laughed, and sat down in a small satin upholstered chair opposite the dowager duchess, all her fears almost forgotten. The duchess was obviously cut from the same easy cloth as her son and daughter, and not a high stickler at all.

That was excellent. Georgina had never fared well with high sticklers.

Emily soon had them all situated with tea and cakes, and tried to tuck her mother's lap robe closer about her.

"Are you quite warm enough, Mother?" she said. "Perhaps I should build up the fire some more."

"I am fine, Em! Do quit fussing, dear." Dorothy smiled at Georgina over her teacup. "I want to hear all about our guest. Emily and I have been reading all the London papers, Mrs. Beaumont, and we understand you are quite famous."

Georgina laughed. "I would not say *famous*. Yet."

"She is being too modest, Mother," said Alex. "Everyone knows who she is, and every family in the *ton* clamors for a portrait by her. Her latest client was Lady Harriet Granville."

Emily's eyes were shining. "Oh, you must tell us all about your life, Mrs. Beaumont! It must be so very exciting to be in London, and on the Continent. I have never even left the neighborhood."

"Oh, but I think *your* life so fascinating!" Georgina protested. "A lovely home like this, being surrounded by people you have always known—it must be so very comfortable. Much more so than my rackety life!"

Dorothy patted her daughter's hand. "We do truly have a lovely home and fine neighbors, Mrs. Beaumont. Yet I fear Emily longs for operas and balls and bookshops."

"Who would not?" Emily sighed. "You must tell me every detail of Town life, Mrs. Beaumont, I beg you."

"Em!" Dorothy scolded. "I fear, Mrs. Beaumont, you will think my daughter quite pushing."

"Not at all," protested Georgina. "I will gladly tell anything you wish to know, since you have been so kind as to share your home with me for a few days. I could even do a small portrait of you, Lady Emily, if you like."

Emily almost bounced on her seat in excitement. "Oh, would you, Mrs. Beaumont! I will be quite the envy of the whole neighborhood."

"It would be my pleasure. You are such a pretty subject! Though I fear it would be a poor effort compared to the painting you have over there."

Georgina nodded toward the portrait that hung above the fireplace. It was a luminous family scene, of a younger Dorothy, a handsome blond gentleman who must be her husband, two little boys, and an infant in pink ruffles. They were gathered beneath a tree, with Fair Oak in the background.

"Is it a Gainsborough?" she asked.

"Yes," answered Dorothy, turning a fond eye on the

painting. "It *is* lovely. That was quite the happiest time of my life, Mrs. Beaumont, with my dearest William and all our little ones. I insisted that we keep it, despite all the . . ." Her voice trailed away, and her gaze fell from the painting to her lap. "I do apologize, Mrs. Beaumont, for chattering on so, when you must be tired from your journey. Emily can show you to your room."

"Thank you, Lady Wayland," Georgina said quietly. "I am a bit tired."

"Alex's bumpy driving is enough to make anyone so!" Emily said, coming over to take Georgina's arm.

"Ah! You see how I am maligned by my family," Alex protested with good humor. "Tell them what an excellent driver I am, I beg you."

"Well," Georgina said consideringly. "You *are* a better driver than I, but as I am always oversetting myself, that can scarce be in your favor."

"You drive yourself, Mrs. Beaumont?" Emily asked in wonder. "I have a pony cart, but that is not very dashing."

"I do have a curricle," Georgina answered. "But I fear I may not drive for a while, as I have had a mishap."

"A mishap?" said Emily.

"Yes, and she is only just recovered," Alex said sternly. "So see that she rests, Em."

"Oh, I shall!" said Emily, drawing Georgina toward the door. "Just as soon as she tells me everything about it."

Dorothy only had time to call out, "We shall see you at supper, then, Mrs. Beaumont," before the door shut, and Emily had Georgina halfway up the stairs.

"Tell me, then, Mother," Alex said, when Georgina and Emily were gone and things were once again settled in the morning room. "What do you think of Mrs. Beaumont?"

Dorothy took a slow sip of her fresh cup of tea. "She is certainly very beautiful."

"Yes. She is."

"We expected no less of her, after all we had read in the newspapers. No doubt she is also quite talented, as well, if people like Hary-O Granville have her paint their portraits." Dorothy glanced up at the treasured Gainsborough, and went on musingly, while Alex sat silently and listened to her. "She has no title. But then, what did an exalted title ever gain us but trouble?"

She laughed humorlessly.

"Her father was the son of a baronet," Alex said.

"Oh, there is no doubt that her connections are *respectable*, I'm sure, or you would have known better than to pursue her seriously. She is wealthy?"

Alex swallowed. "Yes."

"Hm. We do need the blunt, of course. You see how I have been forced to become practical and cynical since your father died?"

"Mother," Alex murmured. "I am so very sorry . . ."

Dorothy laid her hand over her son's. "My dear, do not apologize again, I beg you! There was nothing at all you could have done. The army needed you. You were far away, and your brother, rest his naughty soul, was the duke. There was nothing anyone could have done. You have always been the best of sons to me, and the best of brothers to Emily."

"I have always tried to be."

"And so, I suspect, you will always go on being. You have brought an interesting lady to Fair Oak. She will make you a fine bride, I think."

"Because she is rich?" Alex asked quietly, his jaw taut.

Dorothy shook her head. "Surely you know me better than that? Because you obviously care for her. As your father cared for me, the daughter of an impoverished, gambling wastrel of a viscount."

"I do care for Georgina. Very much. The money only—complicates matters."

"How so? I think that that is your pride talking, but I will not scruple to say that the money will be useful. Without it we could not give Em a proper London Season, which she so deserves. She has looked after me and this estate, has shouldered burdens no young girl should have to." Dorothy paused thoughtfully. "I will admit I had hopes you would look kindly on one of the neighbors' daughters. But it is obvious that you love this Mrs. Beaumont, and I have always wanted nothing but my childrens' happiness. And I suspect she is just the woman to make you happy."

Alex laughed, a profound relief sweeping through him. "I know that she is. And I pray that I can make her happy, as well."

"Oh, I have no doubt that you can! A handsome man such as yourself. I must say I am quite relieved that you did not bring some giggling miss we do not know! We have always been such an eccentric family, I fear we would have shocked such a creature most terribly. The neighbors are used to us, but I am sure London girls would not be."

"Mother! Surely you must know I would never have chosen such a girl for a wife? Why, all the little debutantes looked at me with abject fear that I might ask them to dance, I am so old and weather-beaten."

"I would wager their mamas would have delighted to have you dance with their darlings, an eligible duke like you," Dorothy said with satisfaction. "I would also wager that your Mrs. Beaumont never shrank in 'abject fear' from anything in her life."

"No, she is quite fearless. She is much like you in that respect, Mother."

Dorothy laughed. "Excellent! She will need much courage to take *us* on. Tell me, Alex, does she ride?"

"I am sure she does, though I have not seen her. She drives like a very demon."

"I do like her more and more. Perhaps she would be interested in joining the local hunt, once you are married and settled."

"Now, Mother," Alex warned. "I have not yet made an offer, and when I do it is by no means certain that she will accept."

"Nonsense! She likes you every bit as much as you like her. And now, as we are speaking of the hunt, help me into my infernal chair. I must be changing my frock for supper."

Alex slid his arms around his mother's shoulders and beneath her frail legs, and lifted her easily from her armchair before the fire into her wheeled bath chair. Dorothy Kenton had lost the use of her legs ten years before, when she had been thrown from her horse during a wild hunt.

"I do hope you will like your room," Emily said, leading the way up the stairs and down a dim corridor. "It is our very nicest guest chamber."

"Then, I'm sure I *shall* like it," Georgina answered. "Your whole house is quite lovely."

"It was once," said Emily, with a flash of bitterness. "And the Queen's Room still is. See?"

She threw open a door, and they stepped into an enchanted room.

Georgina could have imagined herself in the Sleeping Beauty's chamber of one hundred years' sleep. The bed of elaborately carved dark wood was enormous, hung about with deep red velvet curtains embroidered in gold. More red draperies hung at the tall windows, making the room into a rich tent beneath the carved ceiling.

A fire danced in a marble grate, while Lady Kate napped before its warmth. Daisy was already unpacking and hanging gowns in the large wardrobe.

"Oh," Georgina sighed. "It *is* grand, Lady Emily."

"Please! Do call me just Emily." Emily sat down beside Lady Kate, and rubbed the ecstatic dog's tummy. "I hope," she went on shyly, "that we shall be friends."

"I know we shall." Georgina tossed her muff, gloves, and hat onto the high bed, and sat next to Emily and Lady Kate. "And you must call me Georgina. Or Georgie, as all my friends do."

"Georgie," Emily repeated. "What a nice name! I cannot tell you how very, very happy I am that you have come here, Georgie. We have not had visitors in such a long time, not since I was a child really."

"Truly? Did your parents or late brother never have company here?"

Emily snorted inelegantly. "Damian *never* came to the country, if he could possibly help it. My parents used to have parties here all the time, until Mother's accident. Things became very quiet then."

"Her accident?"

"Did you not know? She cannot walk. When I was eight years old, there was a riding accident, and she has been confined to her chair ever since. After Damian's death, I became convinced our family is cursed when it comes to horses."

Georgina was shocked. "I confess I had no idea! She seems so healthy."

"Oh, she is! And her mind is sharper than ever. She simply cannot walk. She would be happy to know that you could not tell it; she so hates pity."

"I certainly do not pity her. Rather, I admire her."

"Excellent! For we certainly admire you, you know."

Georgina laughed, causing Lady Kate to sit up and bark at her. "That is most flattering, but how can you admire me when we have only just met?"

"We have read all about you, as I said. The routs you attend, your paintings, your clothes . . ." Emily stood and went to examine the gowns Daisy had laid out on the bed. She carefully touched the skirt of a cream-and-gold striped satin gown. "Your clothes are truly wondrous. Even Lady Anders, our neighbor, has nothing so fine!"

Georgina rose, and came to hold up the gown, measuring it against Emily's blonde curls and fair complexion. "You will have far finer, I am sure, when you make your bow."

Emily shook her head, turning away to examine a violet silk. "Even if I did go to London, I would have nothing so grand. Mother says white is what a young lady wears." She pulled a face. "I loathe white! I should much prefer a gown like this one."

"I quite agree about white; it can be rather insipid, except on a very few fortunate women. I always looked ridiculous in it! But that gown is too old for you. The blue color you are wearing looks very well on you, and would be quite suitable for your age."

Emily shrugged again, obviously uncomfortable with talk of her own attire and forthcoming debut.

Georgina thought it best to change the subject.

"Tell me, why is this room called the Queen's Room?"

Emily brightened a bit. "Because Queen Elizabeth slept here, hundreds of years ago! It was right after she gifted the first duke with his title. She stayed here for four days, and slept in this very bed."

"Truly?" Georgina cried. She kicked off her shoes and clambered onto the bed, climbing over her gowns to lie down full length against the bolsters. "Queen Elizabeth lay right here, where I am now?"

Emily laughed. "Yes! Well, perhaps not *exactly* there, but very near."

"How very exciting! I have never slept in a queen's bed before."

Emily sat next to her, and Lady Kate leaped up to join in the excitement. "It is said that she haunts Fair Oak. That every year, on the anniversary of her stay here, she walks the corridors again."

"Have you ever seen her?"

Emily shook her head. "Never. Though when I was a child, I used to sneak in here every year on the day, to hide under the bed and wait for her. Alas, she never appeared. My brother Damian tried to scare me with tales that *he* had seen her, as well as her headless mother Queen Anne, but I never believed him. He was usually in his cups, you see, and therefore all his visions were suspect."

"And Alex? Did he ever see her?"

Emily laughed. "Dear, military, proud, rational Alex? He, of course, says it is all a Banbury tale."

"Hm. Well, I think it is all quite bone-chilling, like something in a novel. My own house in Italy dates back to medieval times, but I have never heard a report of a ghost there."

Emily looked down at her lap, suddenly shy. "Will you—will you tell me about Italy sometime, Georgie?"

"I will gladly tell you more than you ever wanted to know!" Georgina answered. "I am always eager to talk about my home. But should we not be dressing for supper?"

Emily glanced over at the small clock on the mantle. "I had not realized it had grown so very late! Yes, I must be going. But . . ." Impulsively, the girl kissed Georgina's cheek. "Oh, Georgie, I *am* happy you have come here with my brother."

"So am I, Emily," Georgina answered quietly. "Very happy indeed."

Chapter Thirteen

"What do you think of Fair Oak now, Georgina?" Alex asked as he and Georgina strolled about the overgrown garden after supper.

Georgina turned to look back at the house, serene in the pale moonlight. The doors to the terrace were open, spilling out firelight, and Dorothy and Emily were seated there with their embroidery. It all looked so comfortable and cozy, and in the darkness there was no sign of overgrown ivy or peeling paint.

"I think it is lovely," she answered truthfully. "I do believe it is the first English country house I have ever visited that feels like a true home. Not just a showcase for country weekends, or a place to come shooting."

"It is a home," Alex agreed. "My parents came here soon after they were wed, and seldom lived anyplace else. They only went to their London house for a few weeks every Season, then hurried back. My mother adored the country, where she could be near her horses and her dogs. And her children, of course, though we were a distant third!"

Georgina laughed. "Oh, yes!" They had come to a small summerhouse, and she went inside to sit down on one of the benches. Some of the roof slats were missing, and moonlight fell in silvery bars across the leaf-strewn floor. "Emily told me there were often parties here when she was a child."

Alex sat down beside her, stretching out his long legs before him. "Yes. Just because my parents preferred the country, that does not mean they were in any way unsociable. They belonged to the local hunt—my mother was the only female member for quite a long time. They would give the hunt breakfasts, and the hunt ball. And there was a grand ball every Christmas, which Damian and I, and later Emily, were expected to attend for an hour."

"Only an hour?"

"Quite long enough to gorge ourselves on sweetmeats and make ourselves very ill! Damian especially was rather greedy."

Georgina laughed merrily. "Oh, Alex! It sounds like you had quite a delightful childhood."

"It was delightful. I fear I did not fully appreciate it until much later. During the most difficult times in Spain, it was memories of my family, of life at Fair Oak, that kept me sane."

"Then, I am very glad you have brought me here, and have chosen to share it with me."

Alex smiled down at her, and reached for her hand. "There is no one I would rather share it with than you. You seem such a part of it all, after only one evening."

Georgina curled her fingers around his, wishing that she had not worn gloves, that she could feel his skin against hers. "I wish that were so. I do so admire your home, Alex, and your mother and sister, as well. They are not at all what I expected!"

"What did you expect?"

"Oh, very grand ladies. A dowager duchess and duke's sister, who were high in the instep, and who insisted on all the proprieties. Exactly how the few other duchesses I have met behaved. I was rather anxious."

"You, Georgina? Anxious about a mere duchess? Now that I cannot believe."

"It is absolutely true, I assure you! I wanted so much for them to like me, but I feared they could not, as our lives are so dissimilar."

"Well, I could certainly have reassured you on *that* point. Mother is very like you; she was always very independent, and quite indifferent to the high sticklers. And Emily looks as if she will turn out exactly the same."

"Yes. They are so very *nice*, all that is welcoming! I am very relieved."

"Excellent!" Alex lifted her hand to his lips, his breath warm and sweet through the thin kid of her glove. "Perhaps we should rejoin them?"

Georgina smiled. "Before your mother recalls her duties as chaperone, and sends Emily out here to fetch us?"

"I doubt Mother would care if we stayed out here for hours!" Alex laughed.

"Truly?" Georgina leaned just a bit closer to him, her hand still in his. "Then, perhaps we should."

"Georgina." He stared down at her, his eyes shining and silvery. Then his arms came about her, warm and safe and sheltering. "Blast it all, Georgie, but I cannot be a gentleman one second longer!"

His lips came down to meet hers. Georgina's eyes widened in surprise, then fluttered closed at the delicious warmth that flooded through her like fine brandy. She looped her arms around his neck, burying her fingers in his soft curls as his mouth slanted on hers.

Oh, it had been so long! So very, very long since she had felt this way. So full of love and longing and hope. Not since Jack. Maybe not even then.

And never had she felt so cherished, so safe, as she did now, with Alex Kenton's arms about her.

"Oh, my dears, there you are!" Dorothy called as Alex and Georgina appeared again in the drawing room. "I feared I would have to send a search party after you."

Georgina laughed nervously. She and Alex had carefully straightened their attire and smoothed their hair, but Georgina feared she might still appear scandalously disheveled. Or perhaps her guilt and delight shone in her eyes?

She peeked up at Alex, and he winked at her.

Georgina laughed. She squeezed his arm gently one more time, then went to take a seat before the fire, where Dorothy was still bent over her sewing. "Oh, no, Lady Wayland! Your son was just showing me your lovely garden."

"Lovely? Pah!" answered Dorothy. "It is quite an overgrown tangle. But once it was very nice." She looked over at Georgina slyly. "My husband and I were especially fond of the old summerhouse."

Georgina could feel herself becoming uncomfortably warm—and it had naught to do with the fire. "Oh! Yes. It is very—pretty."

"I knew you would think so." Dorothy set aside her sewing. "Emily and I were just saying we should have a party for you while you are here."

"Oh, yes!" agreed Emily. "It would be such fun."

"A party?" Alex asked doubtfully as he sat down

next to his sister. "I am not certain that would be a good idea."

"Oh, nothing at all grand," Dorothy said quickly. "No great ball or anything of that sort. A great many of our neighbors are in Town, of course, but there are many left who would enjoy some cards, perhaps a little music, an informal supper. I am sure they would delight in meeting the famous Mrs. Beaumont!"

"Oh, yes, Alex, please!" Emily laid her hand on her brother's arm beseechingly. "We have not had anyone here to dine in such a very long time, excepting the vicar and his wife. And we would not want to bore Georgina to death while she is here. She might never come back!"

Alex's doubtful frown turned to a smile then. "Heaven forfend anyone should be bored at Fair Oak!"

"You could scarce bore me at all, Emily," protested Georgina. "And I vow it would take a very great deal of tedium to bore me to death."

"You *should* meet the neighbors, Georgina," said Emily. "Should she not, Alex?"

"Oh, very well," he agreed, much to Emily's bouncing delight. "But no balls!"

"No!" said Dorothy. "Just supper and cards, as I said. We must invite Reverend and Mrs. Upton, of course. And Lord and Lady Anders are still at Thistle Hill, with their daughters. And dear Mr. Arnum . . ."

"Oh, Georgina, I cannot thank you enough!"

Georgina looked over at Emily, who had lit Georgina's way to her bedroom door. "Thank me? Whatever for?"

"For giving us an excuse for a party, of course. It

will not be what you are used to, I fear, but it will be people in the house for you to talk to."

"Nonsense! I am sure it will be vastly agreeable. You must only let me know if I can be of any help in the arrangements."

"Oh, no! You are here to enjoy yourself. Mother and I will see to everything. But perhaps . . ." Emily hesitated.

"Yes?"

"Perhaps—you would loan me a gown? Everyone here has seen my old evening frocks, and Mrs. Jones in the village could never create anything as lovely as your gowns."

Georgina laughed. "Oh, Emily! I would be more than happy to loan you any gown you choose."

"Truly?"

"Truly."

Emily threw her arms about Georgina impulsively, and kissed her cheek. "I *am* glad you have come to Fair Oak, Georgina! Good night."

"Good night, Emily."

As Georgina sat down at her dressing table to remove her earrings and hairpins, she couldn't help but smile at her own reflection in the mirror.

"Yes," she told herself. "I am quite glad I have come to Fair Oak, too."

Chapter Fourteen

Georgina leaned over her sketchbook, tears of helpless laughter streaming from her eyes as she watched Emily cavorting around the morning room with Lady Kate. The two of them raced from one end of the room to the other, Emily holding Lady Kate's chew ball high above her head while the terrier barked wildly. Finally, Lady Kate gained the advantage, leaping up on Emily's skirts and knocking her back onto a chair.

Lady Kate seized the ball, and pranced about victoriously.

"Oh, you naughty dog!" Emily gasped. "Give me back that ball this instant."

Lady Kate replied by laying down, dropping the ball between her forepaws and grinning up at Emily.

Dorothy was giggling into her handkerchief. "Emily Kenton! Here Georgina will think I have raised a hoyden."

"Certainly not," said Georgina. "Lady Kate is impossible to refuse when she wishes to play."

"Indeed she is," answered Emily. "But I am quite done in now, Lady Kate. You must find another playmate. Perhaps you should have gone off to the farm with Alex."

"She would have enjoyed that," Georgina said. "However, she would have made herself impossibly dirty, and been completely unfit for polite society."

"Never! Lady Kate, you will never be unfit for *my* society," Emily protested.

Lady Kate barked joyously, and jumped up into Emily's lap.

"Good girl, Lady Kate!" Georgina praised. "Now, if you will just stay there as you are, I can finish my sketch."

"Oh, yes! Of course." Emily straightened her skirt, and tugged Lady Kate into the proper pose. "Is this right, Georgina?"

"Perfect." Georgina took up her charcoal again.

"You know, I really ought to have gone to the fields with Alex, to tell him what everything is. I have been watching over them these three years," Emily mused. "But this is ever so much more fun!"

"I should hope so!" Dorothy cried. "I never liked you mucking about the farm, even if there was no one else for it. And you should be helping with the guest list for our supper." She waved about the sheaf of lists she had been bent over on her lap desk.

"Oh, Mother, you are doing an excellent job all on your own," said Emily. "I do think, though . . ."

"Sh!" said Georgina. "I am trying to capture just the right curve of your cheek, Emily. No talking at present, if you please."

"Of course," replied Emily, then snapped her jaw shut.

Lady Kate barked.

"You must be quiet, too, Lady Kate," admonished Georgina.

Lady Kate lowered her muzzle to her paws with a sigh.

Georgina resumed her work, humming a happy little tune as she traced the pretty lines of Emily's face. She had been quite absurdly happy ever since she had woken that morning, and had floated through her toilette and breakfast. She had soared when Alex kissed her hand before he rode out, and she still felt rather light and silly as the morning moved toward luncheon.

And all because a man had kissed her in the moonlight!

But not just any man—Alex. Alex had kissed her!

She had not felt so very giddy over a mere kiss since Jack Reid had slipped her behind the chicken house at Miss Thompson's School, and placed his lips on hers so quickly and furtively.

She had been almost eighteen then. She was thirty now, almost thirty-one. Surely it was quite absurd for a woman of her years to be so giddy over a mere kiss!

Yet it had not been just any kiss. It had been wonderfully thrilling, and sweet, and dear. Surely she deserved this happiness, this moment of soaring delight? Surely she had earned it with all her years of loneliness.

Yes. Of course she had!

"Of course," she murmured aloud.

"Did you say something, Georgina?" Dorothy asked.

Georgina looked up from her sketch, startled. "What? Oh, no. I just have the tendency to talk to myself when I am working. It is of no matter."

"Ah. Well, I think I have finished our guest list at last!" Dorothy straightened her papers with an air of great satisfaction. "I do so want everything to be perfect. This will be our first supper here in a long time."

"Of course it will be perfect, Mother," said Emily, shifting a bit in her chair. "How can it help but be?"

Later that afternoon, when Dorothy and Lady Kate had gone off to take an après-luncheon nap, Georgina and Emily sat out on the sunlit terrace to play a game of Beggar My Neighbor.

As Emily turned over a queen, and Georgina handed over two of her own cards, Emily said, "It must be great fun to be in Town at this time of year."

Georgina shrugged. "I suppose it is, yes. There are certainly a great many balls and routs, and it is very good for my business! But I will tell you truly, Emily, the balls are generally so very crowded one can scarce breathe, let alone move or talk."

"Is there nothing fun about it?"

"To be sure! Gunter's has delicious ices, and there is always someone dressed absurdly at the opera to lend amusement. But I really only go there to see my dear friends, the Hollingsworths."

"Lady Elizabeth Hollingsworth? Who is an artist, too?"

"Yes. We met at school, and have been good friends ever since."

"We often read of her and her husband in the papers. I should so much like to meet her."

"And so you shall! I am sure the two of you would like each other very much."

Emily handed over three cards when Georgina turned over a king, and said slowly, "I suppose you prefer Italy to England."

"In many ways I do. It is warmer there, for one," Georgina laughed.

"Then, you would not care to marry an Englishman?"

Georgina looked up from her cards, surprised. She had not at all seen where this conversation was leading. Was Emily afraid Georgina would not marry Alex? Or was she afraid that Georgina *would*? "I think that I would perhaps feel differently if I had family in England."

Emily nodded, apparently satisfied. "I am sure you have many suitors in London."

"A few," Georgina answered carefully. "Though I would scarce call them *suitors*. Admirers, perhaps. None that I would take seriously."

"How lovely it must be to have so many admirers," Emily said wistfully as she sorted through the cards she had won.

"But you must have every young swain of the neighborhood at your feet. Such a lovely girl as yourself," answered Georgina. "I wager you could have your choice."

Emily shook her head. "We don't often have the chance to go to an assembly or a supper. And when we do, there is a distinct lack of eligible beaux!" She laughed. "There is always Arthur Hoenig, of course. His father would be more than happy to be allied with the Kentons, but unfortunately, poor Arthur has smelly breath and spots!"

Georgina laughed in turn. "Oh, Emily! I know you must have better prospects than that. Is there no young man you find to your liking? No one handsome and charming?"

"Well . . ." Emily hesitated. "Once there was— someone. But that was long ago. I was just a child."

"Really? Will you tell me about it?"

Emily nodded. "When I was just twelve, our neighbor, the Earl of Darlinghurst, returned from India, where he had been for many years."

"And you admired this earl?"

Emily's eyes widened. "The earl? Lud, no! He was fifty if he was a day, and sunburned to a crisp. It was his son. David."

"Ah. I see. You had a *tendre* for this David?"

"Not a *tendre*; I was just a child, of course. He was practically grown up, and scarce noticed me, except to pull my braid and tease me a bit. But he was so very handsome, quite the most handsome man I had ever seen. He had a voice like—like nothing I had ever heard. So rich and sweet, like a cup of chocolate."

"What happened?"

"It was a great scandal. You see, the earl had married an Indian woman. The daughter of a maharaja, so they said. She had died soon after their son was born. So David was half-Indian."

"No!" Georgina gasped, fascinated.

"Yes. I fear it was not quite comfortable for them in the neighborhood. He was an earl, so people felt they *had* to receive them, of course. But they were not exactly friendly to them, especially David. My parents stood as their only true friends. I believe that is why they returned to India, after little more than a year here."

"And you have never forgotten this David?"

Emily shrugged. "We are rather isolated here, and I have few chances to meet such fascinating young men. It was only a schoolgirl crush, really, and I have not seen him since he left. I do not even know where he is now; far away in India, I am sure."

Dorothy, refreshed from her nap, came out onto the terrace, wheeled by her maid. "What are you speaking of so intently, my dears?" she said.

"I was only telling Georgina about the Earl of Darlinghurst, Mother," answered Emily.

"Oh, yes," said Dorothy. "What a charming gentleman he was! And such a handsome young son. William and I were so sad when they left the neighborhood, as I'm sure was Emily. Weren't you, dear?"

"Oh, yes, Mother. Very sad. Quite desolate at not having young David to pull my braids anymore."

"Such a great pity they did not stay to see you grown up." Dorothy opened up her lap desk, and drew out some fresh lists. "Now, my dears, to important business. I have finished the guest list, but we must begin the menus. I do not really think we need forty or fifty removes, as I have read they have at Carlton House, but I do want there to be a choice. And we should have oysters . . ."

"Where shall we find oysters at this time of year, Mother?" interrupted Alex, striding out onto the terrace, still in his riding clothes.

"The fishmonger in the village will have plenty, of course, Alexander," she replied as he bent to kiss her cheek. "We are scarcely living in the middle of nowhere, though it sometimes feels that way. And you are very dusty, dear."

"I apologize, Mother. I was on my way upstairs to wash when I heard you all talking out here. I wanted to see what you are so merry about."

Alex kissed Emily's cheek, and bowed over Georgina's hand. He *was* rather dusty, with mud on his boots and a slightly earthy smell about his coat. But Georgina thought she had never seen anything quite so lovely as his windswept hair and tanned, whisker-roughened jaw.

He smiled down at her warmly.

"We were discussing the supper your mother is to

give," Georgina answered him, with a smile of her own.

"Of what else could we be speaking?" said Emily. "And Georgina has quite beggared me! You see, she has taken all my cards."

Chapter Fifteen

The day of the planned supper began warm and sunny. Emily even rode out to the fields with Alex, and Dorothy sequestered herself in the dining room with her maid, to see to the final arrangements. She shooed Georgina outside to the gardens, insisting that she needed no help.

So Georgina took her sketchbook and went back to the summerhouse, where she had kissed Alex so sweetly. That night it had been dark, and she had not been able to see anything but their immediate surroundings. Today the sun was bright, and she had a full view of the gardens and the back of the house.

It was a pleasing sight, despite the tangles of the flower beds and the spots of peeling paint. It was peaceful and calm, settled.

All the things Georgina was not, and had always longed to be.

Could she, despite her dreamings, really ever be a proper mistress to such a place? A proper duchess? She knew that her money would be useful to the Kentons, to Fair Oak. But could she *herself* be useful to them?

Georgina chewed on her thumbnail, an old nervous habit, as old doubts rose up to plague her. When she was a child, living under her aunt and uncle's cold care, she had often been told that she was unworthy. That she was wild, completely lacking in decorum and natural grace and beauty. That who she was was in no way good enough for polite society.

She had fought down those insecurities with years of self-sufficiency and success in her chosen work. She knew that people admired her, even thought her beautiful. They thought her dashing and sophisticated.

But that did not mean that she had completely fought back that frightened young girl. She still rose up to plague the grown-up Georgina from time to time.

As she did now, when Georgina was contemplating what it would be like to be a duchess.

"Nonsense!" she cried aloud. "I would be a perfect duchess. Top of the trees."

She snapped open her sketchbook, flipped over to the almost completed sketch of Emily, and began to do what she knew she did best. She drew.

"Now. Which gown would you like to wear?" Georgina threw open her wardrobe to Emily's perusal.

Emily's eyes grew wide as she looked at first one gown then another. "I—I hardly know where to begin." She took up the gold-embroidered green velvet that Georgina had worn at the first ball she attended with Alex. "This one?"

Georgina studied it critically. "It doesn't really suit your lovely blonde hair. Perhaps this one?" She showed Emily a gown of pale peach satin, overlaid with soft ivory lace. "I have never worn it. It suits you so much better than me!"

"Oh, yes," Emily sighed happily, clutching the gown to her. "May I, please, Georgina? It is quite the loveliest thing I have ever seen."

"Of course you may!"

"And what will you wear?"

"The blue silk, I think. Do you think it quite appropriate?"

"I think you will be stunning. We will be the envy of all our neighbors, to have such a lovely and famous guest."

Georgina laughed. "You will be the envy of your neighbors because you are so lovely yourself! Sit here, Emily, and I will fix your hair for you. There is a new style I have seen in Town that I think will suit you admirably."

Emily sat down before the dressing table mirror, and watched with sparkling eyes as Georgina brushed out her curls and began twisting them atop her head. "I have a white rose I picked in the garden this afternoon," she said. "Would that look well in my hair? I fear I have so few jewels."

"It would be perfect. Tell me, Emily, how was your afternoon? Did you ride far?"

"Oh, yes! I showed Alex all the fields that are under cultivation, and a few that I hope to have plowed in the fall. Poor man, he does not know a great deal about farming as yet! He is such a military man. But he is learning."

Alex was utterly exhausted.

He and Emily had been out all afternoon. He had seen the fields (few) that Emily had managed to keep under cultivation. He had seen the fields (many) that lay fallow. Emily had talked of possible plans for those fields, of barley and wheat and bringing in more sheep.

They had spoken with the tenants, had heard their concerns and advice.

Alex had learned more about farming in one day than he ever had before in his life, and he felt like an utter babe in the woods. As a younger son, he had been meant for the army since childhood. Thus his father had not thought it important for him to know about the running of the estates. But he intended to know everything about it now, and soon.

He also learned that his sister, only a child when he had left for Spain, had grown into a beautiful young woman. A very smart young woman, who had taught herself about farming when her brothers were nowhere about to see to her welfare. She had kept Fair Oak in good order, and looked after their mother, at the expense of all the normal pleasures of a young lady.

Emily knew so little of parties and suitors; she had few friends of her own age. She was clearly longing for those joys; she spoke so wistfully of London.

It was no wonder she had attached herself so quickly to Georgina's friendship.

Alex owed Emily that friendship, owed her a fine Season, at the very least, for all she had done. His mother would never want to go to London again, so he owed Emily a grand sponsor. He owed her, and himself, to learn all he could about soil cultivation and sheep shearing, so that he could build the Grange into a kingdom any woman would be proud to be duchess of.

Even a woman as glorious as Georgina Beaumont.

Alex grinned at himself in the mirror as he finished off his cravat. Georgina *would* make a splendid duchess. He had known that in London, and seeing her here in his home, seeing how easy and friendly she was with his mother and sister, only proved that.

Yes, he admitted to himself, he quite adored Georgina.

If he could just be worthy of her.

"Reverend Mr. Upton! Mrs. Upton. You must meet our new houseguest, Mrs. Beaumont," called Dorothy from where she sat in the drawing room, greeting the guests before supper. As she smiled and chatted, her cheeks pink beneath the lappets of her lace cap, she looked no older than the woman in the Gainsborough portrait.

"A great pleasure, Mrs. Beaumont," said the vicar, a tall, thin, smiling man. "We saw a portrait you did of a friend of my aunt's, a Lady Treezle. Quite fine, was it not, Mrs. Upton?"

"Oh, quite!" agreed Mrs. Upton, a pretty blonde as short and plump as her husband was the opposite. "It was very like her, Mrs. Beaumont. We were so excited to hear that you were in the neighborhood."

"Thank you, Mrs. Upton," answered Georgina. "I have had such a delightful welcome from everyone."

"You must come to tea at the vicarage before you leave," Mrs. Upton urged.

"I should like that very much, thank you." As the Uptons went on to speak to Dorothy about some new ladies' charitable organization, Georgina stepped away a bit to survey the room.

She had rather feared that her pearl necklace with its sapphire pendant and the sapphire bandeau that held her hair in place would prove too much for a country party. But she saw now that all the ladies wore their finest gowns and their prettiest jewels; Lady Anders even wore a tiara! And quite all the country gentry had flocked to the dowager duchess's supper party, obviously eager to be at Fair Oak again. There was much conversation and laughter, and everyone had greeted her warmly, and even with a touch of deference.

Deference was something Georgina was not accustomed to in the least, and she suspected that was entirely due to Alex's behavior. He had stayed at her side as the first of the guests arrived, introduced her about.

She smiled at him now, where he stood with his sister and a few other people. He smiled at her in return, and nodded. Then he winked.

There was a small fluttering, very low in her stomach. She almost giggled, and clapped her gloved hand to her mouth.

"Georgina, dear," Dorothy said, bringing Georgina back to her side. "I do believe it is time for supper. Will you ask Alexander to come and assist me?"

"Yes, of course," she answered. "Do excuse me, Mr. Upton. Mrs. Upton."

"Of course, Mrs. Beaumont." The vicar gave her a bow.

As she walked away, Georgina heard Dorothy say, "You see how very much livelier we are since Mrs. Beaumont came to visit? Emily has quite blossomed. Such a treasure."

"Yes," said Mr. Upton. "You—and your son— appear to be quite happy in your friends, Your Grace."

Georgina blushed.

"An excellent port, Wayland," Lord Anders commented. "Most excellent indeed."

"Thank you," answered Alex. "I sent it back from Spain."

The ladies had retired to the drawing room, leaving the gentlemen to their port and cigars.

"Shows your excellent taste," Anders said, with a suggestive chuckle. "In port as in other things, eh?"

"Other things?"

"Women, of course, Wayland! La Beaumont. We have only recently come up from Town, you know, and she is all the crack there. A true beauty, and so dashing." Anders laughed, bringing the attention of the others in their direction. "What other woman would challenge old Lord Pynchon to a race, eh!"

There was an answering ripple of laughter. "She *is* a stunner," commented young Baron Patterson. "That hair . . . !"

Alex glared at Anders, just as he had to many an errant subaltern on the Peninsula. It had the same effect on Anders as it had on them—he stammered a bit, turned red, and shifted his gaze away.

All the others turned back to their respective conversations.

"You know, of course," said Alex, "that Mrs. Beaumont was injured in that race. I hardly think she would appreciate that it has now become an object of laughter."

"Oh—yes. I mean, no," murmured Anders. "But—but she does seem quite recovered now."

"She is recovered. Quite. It is still not something to be snickered over, however."

"Oh, no! I was not—snickering. Merely expressing my admiration for her."

"Hm. Yes."

Anders took a long sip of his port, and seemed to recover himself. "I take it, then, Wayland, that your feelings toward La—Mrs. Beaumont are of a rather serious nature?"

Alex was quite taken aback. Surely such bluntness was not quite the thing? It had certainly not been before he left for war; people had at least outwardly minded their own business. But then, he had been gone a long time. And, as he did not wish his feelings for Georgina to be in any way misconstrued, he said, "I brought her here to meet my mother and sister."

"Certainly." Anders drank down the last of his port. "Well, I must say you are a very fortunate man, Wayland. She is beautiful, and, I hear, quite well-to-do." He glanced toward the sideboard, now all but bare of silver where once it had groaned from the weight of salvers and platters. "*Quite* well-to-do."

Alex's hand tightened on his own glass. He only released his grip when he felt the etched design pressing into his palm and the crystal start to give.

Money again. Always the blasted money. Was this what he could look forward to for all his future married life?

"We were all so delighted to hear that you had come to visit, Mrs. Beaumont." Lady Anders, a tall brunette made even taller by the great plumes attached to her ruby tiara, seated herself next to Georgina with a smile. "And now to have the chance to meet you *and* see Fair Oak again! Beyond delight."

Georgina smiled in return, even though there was something in Lady Anders' eyes she was rather wary of. Some sort of—malicious glitter. "I am delighted to be here."

"Though you must find it a bit dull after all your triumphs in Town," Lady Anders whispered confidingly. "I know I find the society rather limited."

"Limited? With a ducal family in residence?"

Lady Anders laughed. "Oh, yes, the Kentons *are*

highly regarded, to be sure. But they have been so quiet since Damian—that is, the late duke—died. The dowager duchess and poor Lady Emily haven't an ounce of his dash!" She sighed. "Not that we ever saw him here in the country. We almost always met in Town."

Georgina carefully studied Lady Anders. Obviously she had been more than acquaintances with the profligate Damian—despite the fact that she was old enough to have two daughters out. "Indeed," Georgina said coolly.

Lady Anders took no note of the frosty tone. "Yes. Fair Oak is so *shabby* without him, quite without style. Though I must say Lady Emily looks in fine form tonight. Is that a new gown even? Quite unusual. She usually takes no interest in fashion at all. Though I have tried to advise her in such things, for her brother's sake, she does not care."

Georgina looked across the room to where Emily, so pretty in her peach satin and ivory lace, was playing whist with her mother and the Uptons. Emily laughed, a sweet sound, like silver bells a bit rusty from disuse. She looked so happy, and so young.

Georgina thought of how many difficulties that young girl had been through, all because her late brother had squandered her fortune. Squandered it with the woman who now sat beside Georgina, sighing about Damian's lost "dash" and Emily's lack of style.

Georgina wanted to flee, but she only nodded and said, "Lady Emily *is* looking well tonight. She is a very lovely young lady. And if Fair Oak is indeed 'shabby,' surely it is only because your Damian took no interest in it."

Lady Anders looked at her, with wide, startled dark

eyes. "Well." Then she looked over to where Alex sat, watching them over his fanned cards. "I see."

Georgina followed her gaze, and saw that Alex was frowning slightly. He seemed uncertain, perhaps even angry.

Why would he be angry?

"Well," Lady Anders continued. "Now I suppose Alexander has returned, he will—take an interest. As, I see, have you, Mrs. Beaumont." Lady Anders looked pointedly at Georgina's sapphires and pearls. "And very fortunate the Kentons are to have your interest. I am sure they must find you quite *useful*. But, if you will excuse me, Mrs. Beaumont, I do believe my husband is calling me."

Georgina nodded briefly. "Of course. So interesting to meet you, Lady Anders."

Georgina watched Lady Anders walk away, her crimson and gold train trailing like a glittering serpent behind her. Lady Anders stopped at her husband's side, whispered in his ear, gestured toward Georgina. He, in turn, nodded, and whispered back to her.

Georgina turned away with a laugh. What a thoroughly irritating wench!

Was she to be plagued with such sordid speculations for all her future married life?

"Mrs. Beaumont."

Georgina turned to see the kindly Mrs. Upton. "Mrs. Upton! Did I not see you playing at cards?"

"Oh, I am terrible at it! I gave the young baron my place."

"I fear I am not a dab hand at cards, myself. Please, won't you sit with me? I find myself in need of some *pleasant* conversation."

"Yes, I saw you were talking with Lady Anders."

"Indeed I was."

Mrs. Upton leaned toward Georgina, her pretty, round face serious, and said quietly, "I know that as a vicar's wife I should show charity to all. But you should not take heed of anything that woman says, my dear. She is a viper, plain and simple."

Georgina could not have agreed more.

Georgina stayed awake that night long after the guests departed and the rest of the household was asleep.

She had been alone for so very long that the new feelings of that evening, feelings of family and neighborhood, felt so strange. She sat beside her bedroom window, looking down at the moonlight-drenched garden, trying to absorb them.

Oh, she had not been strictly *alone* in the many years since Jack died. She had her dear friends, who were like family to her. She had had Mr. Beaumont, who, despite his advanced years, had been a good friend to her. She had her sweet doggie. But she had lived mostly by herself, had gone where she pleased, and had done what she wanted. She had never given the words of vipers like Lady Anders a thought before.

And she liked it. Very much. She did not dwell on things that could not be helped, like Jack's death, or the deep, secret yearning she had felt for a child, a home, and a more secure place in Society.

She had a career, after all. Financial security. She was so fortunate, really.

Georgina sighed. How could she have known, when the handsome Duke of Wayland rescued Lady Kate from drowning, that her life was changing so much from that moment on? That her old yearnings for a home and a family would rise up again? That Alex would show her a world she could so easily live in, one that had once seemed so far beyond her grasp? A world of family and home and lineage. Of complete security and respectability.

Yet so he had. She liked his mother and sister very much. They might be the widow and daughter of a duke, but she sensed in them a kindred spirit to her own. They had, all three of them, been through difficult circumstances, circumstances beyond their control, and had emerged intact. Perhaps even better than before.

She had had fears, before she met them, that they would disapprove of her, perhaps even snub her. That they would have little in common, and this visit would prove a misery. After all, she was hardly the sort a duke would usually consider for a wife.

But those fears had not been realized.

Even the neighbors, who no doubt held the honor of their ducal friends very high, had welcomed her. Perhaps a few had seemed a bit puzzled, but everyone had been civil and charming.

Except the Anders, Georgina amended wryly.

And then there was Alex himself.

Georgina smiled softly. Dear Alex, so handsome, so considerate, so military-proud but so kindhearted. She had wanted him so very much from that first day they met. But she had not wanted him just as an admirer, or even as a lover. She had wanted to talk with him, to sit quietly with him, to dance at balls and drive in the park with him. She wanted to show him all her work, to bask in his approval as she had the night of Elizabeth's *salon*. She wanted to hear of all his experiences in the war; she wanted to know all his hopes for the future.

Chapter Sixteen

"Oh, Georgina! Such dreadful news." Emily rushed up to Georgina as she entered the breakfast room the morning after the supper party.

Georgina's gaze flew to Alex, where he sat with his plate of kippers and eggs. She noticed that Dorothy was not at her place. "Dreadful news? Is someone ill? Has your mother . . . ?"

Alex shook his head. "Not at all! Really, Emily, you should not be so dramatic. You have convinced poor Georgina that someone has died at the very least. It is not so very *dreadful*." He smiled at Georgina, and came around the table to draw her chair out for her. "Please, both of you, do sit, or your food will grow cold."

Emily sat down, disgruntled. "It is dreadful to me, Alex. We have only had you back for a few days, and now you are leaving us again."

"Leaving?" Georgina cried, aghast that her country idyll, so very perfect only last night, was ending so abruptly. "Where are you going?"

"To Kenton Grange, our estate to the north," Alex answered. "I received a letter from the bailiff only this morning. There is an emergency there that I must go and see to at once." He gestured toward the letter beside his plate. "The Grange is our only other estate besides Fair Oak. Once I have seen it to rights, it can be a dowry for Emily."

"Since I intend to never marry, I shall not need a dowry!" protested Emily. "Therefore you should stay here with us for a few days more."

"I shall not be gone long, Em," Alex answered. "A week, perhaps."

Georgina buttered her toast industriously to cover her disappointment. "I shall be ready to return to London this afternoon, then. I suppose a carriage could be hired in the village?"

"Not you, too!" sighed Emily.

"You must stay, Georgina," Alex said quickly. "I promised you a holiday, which you have scarce had. I would not want to ruin your fun, or that of my sister."

"Oh, yes!" Emily beseeched. "Please do stay, Georgina. I could show you about the farm, and we could call on all the neighbors. And you have not seen the village."

A few more days in the country quiet *did* sound tempting. But would it be quite proper without Alex? "I do not know . . ."

"Georgina! Please," cried Emily.

"I should feel too guilty if I sent you running back to London so quickly, Georgina," Alex said. "I will take you back as soon as I return. Or, if you find your work calls you back to Town before then, you could hire a carriage."

Georgina smiled. "Very well. I will stay for a few days more."

Emily clapped her hands. "Oh, how grand! We *shall* miss you, though, Alex."

"Yes," Georgina agreed. "We certainly shall."

"I will not be gone long enough for you to miss me," Alex protested. "You will be having far too much fun without me. But I know that *I* will miss *you*."

"Are you certain you will be comfortable here while I am gone?" Alex asked Georgina as he prepared to climb aboard his curricle. "If you feel we bullied you into staying, and you really want to return to Town, you mustn't let us hold you."

Georgina laughed. "Not at all! I am glad to have more time to spend here, in your lovely home."

"Good." He laid his hand softly against her cheek. "I am truly sorry to leave you thus. I would never do so if it were not an emergency."

"Of course not! You must safeguard your sister's dowry. I shall do very well here with Emily and your mother."

"I know you will." Alex glanced about at the house, shimmering in the morning sunlight, then down at Georgina. She looked so very *right* there. As if she had been living there for years. As if she belonged.

He leaned forward to kiss her cheek, but longed for so much more.

"I will write to you," he murmured against her soft skin. "As soon as I arrive at the Grange."

"And I will write to you. Have a safe journey, Alex."

He looked into her luminous green eyes, at the slight tremble of her lips as she smiled at him, and he longed to pull her into his arms. To kiss her properly. But he was all too aware of his mother and sister, watching avidly from the window.

He knew they would like it all too well if he were

to make a lascivious cake of himself in their very driveway, but he was not quite prepared to be their morning amusement! So he just took up Georgina's hand, and kissed her ungloved fingers, lingering just an instant longer than was proper.

"Good-bye, Georgie," he said, then swung himself up onto the narrow curricle seat and lifted the reins.

"Farewell, Alex. Drive carefully! More carefully than I!"

Alex laughed. Then he waved once more to his mother and sister, and drove away.

As his day's drive was a long one, and he was alone with no one to converse with, he was left with a great deal of time for thinking. And his thoughts turned mostly to Georgina.

Georgina, so beautiful, so charming. She had certainly wrapped his family and all their neighbors about her pretty finger! He smiled to remember her with his mother and sister, how she had made them laugh with her tales of London and the Continent. She had had the neighbors fascinated, as well, and quite admiring of her—just as she had all of London Society at her feet.

She would truly make a magnificent duchess. He was just fortunate that she seemed to admire him, as well, crusty old military man that he was. Otherwise she would surely spurn his suit! All he had to offer her was a tumbledown estate. And Emily would surely kill him now if he did not present Georgina to her as her sister.

Just look at how she had helped Emily, loaning her a fashionable gown so she would look so grand at their supper . . .

He frowned a bit at the reminder that his sister had

required the loan of a gown at all. He should have been able to provide her with an entire wardrobe!

And that, once again, chafed. Georgina's money.

Alex was a proud man. It was his greatest downfall, and he admitted it. It would perhaps be different if he did not care for Georgina so. If he had met a woman he rather liked, who wanted to be a duchess and who was willing to trade her fortune for it, a woman who wanted only a business arrangement. Then he would not mind so much.

But he loved Georgina. So he wanted everything equal and aboveboard between them. He wanted her life to be as fine with him as it had been without him. He wanted her to never have any regrets that she had chosen him.

Could that be possible, when he had so little to offer her?

Lord Anders's words of the night before came back to haunt him. "She is beautiful, and, I hear, quite well-to-do. *Quite* well-to-do."

Alex saw again in his mind's eye the man's odious sneer.

Anders had been right, though, in his own nasty way. Why would a wealthy woman like Georgina, a beautiful, independent woman, want to take on a family that was so messed up? No woman in her situation would.

But then, Georgina was not just any beautiful, wealthy woman. She was his own unique Georgina. And she seemed to like him. Her kisses were sweet and ardent; she smiled brightly whenever he entered a room. She listened to him, confided in him.

He knew he should let her go, for her own good. He could not, though. He had come to rely on their time together. He was being selfish, he knew that, but he could not give her up.

Despite the difficulties that could lie ahead for them, despite the fact that he was more confused than he had ever been before in his life, he could not bring himself to let her go.

"I am just going out to visit Mrs. Smith, our old nursemaid, who has been ill," Emily said, putting on her bonnet and gloves before the mirror in the morning room. "Would you like to come, too, Georgina?"

Georgina, who had been sketching before the fire and chatting with Dorothy, said, "Oh, I should like to, Emily! Fresh air sounds wonderful. But I should finish this sketch today so that I can finish your portrait before I leave Fair Oak."

"Nonsense," said Dorothy. "There will be plenty of time for finishing portraits later, I am sure." She winked, looking so much like her son that Georgina had to laugh. "Plenty of time. You two should go out into the sunshine, while we still have it. Give my best wishes to Mrs. Smith."

"If you are sure, Dorothy, that you will be quite all right?"

"Oh, yes. I have been intending to finish my book."

Georgina smiled. "Then, I should very much like to go with you, Emily. Let me fetch my bonnet, and we can be off."

Twenty minutes later, they set off in Emily's little pony cart, with Emily competently at the reins, and Lady Kate beside them.

"Most of the fields lie fallow now, of course," Emily said, drawing up the pony cart so Georgina could take a closer look at their surroundings. "A great many of the laborers have had to find other work. We have managed to keep on enough to cultivate those fields over there, though."

Georgina surveyed the recently harvested fields. "What is grown there?"

"Wheat and oats. We used to grow barley, as well. There are some turnips and potatoes just over that hill, and cook keeps an excellent kitchen garden. We are never short of vegetables! And I have kept a few head of cattle, to pull the plows and give us milk and some meat. Only enough for the household, though." Emily's rosebud mouth pursed thoughtfully. "I would like to have some sheep, as well, but they cost dear just now."

"Do you still have many tenants?"

"Oh, yes, some. You will meet some of them today, I am sure. Their rents are very welcome, though I wish we could do more for them. They have been a great help to Mother and me, teaching me about farming and livestock." Emily laughed. "I would not have known a plow from a turnip before last year!"

"What of your bailiff?"

"Mr. Pryor? He left soon after Damian died. When I looked over the books after his hasty departure, I found he had been skimming off the top a bit. So good riddance, I say! I've done better without him. Mr. Montgomery, one of the tenants, helps me a bit."

Georgina was shocked. "Do you mean to say, Emily, that you have been managing this farm all by yourself?"

Emily seemed surprised at Georgina's surprise. "Yes. There was no one else to do it. Mother is not well. Alex, although he left the army as soon as he got my letter about Damian's death, was delayed several times, and did not make it home for many months. And he is a military man, not a farmer; he knew as little as I did. I could not just let us starve."

"So you knew nothing of farming when you started?"

Emily shrugged blithely. "Not a thing! French and needlework were all my governess taught me. But I read everything I could find, and asked all our tenants and neighbors for advice. We have not done too badly, considering."

"I should say not." Georgina looked out at the fields again, in complete awe that this young girl, this duke's daughter, had managed them all on her own. She had been worried about wheat and drainage and soil cultivation, when she should have been enjoying her first Season.

If only there was something Georgina could do to help Emily, to help Alex and his family . . .

"Emily," she said. "I have always lived in cities and towns, and I know nothing of farming. How much would it take to put all your fields under cultivation again, and to bring in a new bailiff, an honest one?"

Emily's forehead creased in thought. When she at last named a sum, Georgina said in surprise, "Truly? I would have thought it a great deal more."

"Oh, we could *use* a great deal more, to be sure. The roof on Fair Oak needs repairing, the garden restoring, and, as I said, I should like to bring in sheep. But to hire a new bailiff, and bring the laborers back in time for hay making in a few weeks and then fall plowing, that should do it."

"Hm." Georgina opened her reticule and drew out the thick wad of banknotes she had been intending to use for some shopping in the village. It was quite embarrassing now, to think of the sums she spent on bonnets and slippers. She tucked them into Emily's market basket. "Take this, then, and use it on the roof, or the plowing, or whatever you see fit. I will write you a draught on the rest when we return to the house."

"What!" Emily cried, staring down at the money in shock. "Georgina, what are you doing? You cannot just give me your money! It—it would not be right." But she reached out one hand, in its mended glove, to touch the notes.

"Emily, please. Please, I want to help. I want to cease being a selfish creature, and help do something truly useful."

"It is so good of you, but—to give me, an almost stranger, your money . . ."

Georgina took Emily's hand, and spoke to her quietly, earnestly. "I will tell you something that mustn't go beyond us just yet."

Emily's eyes widened. "What is it?"

"I love your brother, very much, and I am almost certain he loves me, as well. He has asked me to marry him—or as good as asked. And I will say yes."

"Oh!" Emily cried in delight, throwing her arms about Georgina's neck. "I knew it. I knew it from the way he always looks at you. Oh, I will be the envy of the neighborhood, when they hear I am to have such a dashing sister!"

"So, since I *am* to be your sister, let me help you."

"But . . ."

"Emily. My money shall be yours soon enough. But I am not sure when we will be married, and you need the money now, to bring back the laborers. Please."

Emily bit her lip, clearly torn. Then she nodded. "Yes. Georgina, you are the dearest dear! My brother is so very fortunate to have found you."

"Yes," Georgina agreed. "So he is."

Emily laughed.

The next three days passed most pleasantly. Georgina went driving with Emily, took tea with the vicar's wife, and sat and read with Dorothy in the afternoons. She finished the sketches for Emily's portrait, and began laying it down on canvas in oils. In the evenings, she would play cards with Emily and Dorothy, or listen to Emily play on the pianoforte.

Secretly, Georgina began to make plans for the grand Season she would sponsor for Emily. She had never ushered a young girl through her first Season before, but surely it could not be so difficult for a girl as pretty and wellborn as Emily. There would be a presentation at Court, of course, a coming-out ball, routs and breakfasts and musicales . . .

These plans were occupying her on the third night, as she lay awake in bed, when she heard a noise. A light scratching sound.

Georgina cautiously raised her head from the pillow to look about. There was only the familiar furniture visible in the dying firelight. Her gown draped over a chair, where she had dropped it after supper. The only sound was Lady Kate's light snoring.

Then it came again. A faint scratching in the corridor.

Georgina recalled Emily's tales of Queen Elizabeth, who once a year came back to wander about her bed-chamber of more than two hundred years ago.

She sank back down against the pillow, drawing the sheet up to her neck.

"W-who is it?" she called, deliciously chilled. "Do you bring me a message from the other side?"

The door opened, and a blonde head popped into

the room. Very solid, and not at all ghostly. "The other side?" Emily whispered. "The other side of the wall, mayhap, since my room is right next to yours!"

Georgina giggled. "Emily! I thought you were Queen Elizabeth."

"Me? Certainly not. I have no ruff."

"What are you doing wandering about in the middle of the night?"

"I was hungry, so I thought I would go down to the kitchen and see if there was any lemon cake left from tea. Would you like to come with me?"

"I do feel a bit peckish. Contact with the spirit world will do that to a person."

The kitchen was quite deserted when they went down there, and found the lemon cake and some milk. They took their feast back to Georgina's room, and settled down before the fire to eat it. Even Lady Kate got a small portion.

"Do you often make midnight forays into the kitchen?" Georgina asked, scraping up the last of her cake crumbs.

Emily shook her head. "No, but I did when I was a child. Cook would leave little treats out for me, a cake or the last of a meat pie. Sometimes Alex would go with me, though he was quite a bit older and very dignified."

"Did you have a good childhood here, Emily?"

"Oh, yes! The very best." Emily smiled softly at the memory. "My father was sometimes gone, of course, to take his seat in the House of Lords, but when he came back he would bring grand presents, and would take me out riding on my pony every day. He and my mother adored parties, and gave ever so many. Breakfasts, and balls, and suppers. Damian was almost never at home, but I scarcely missed him, he teased me so horridly when he was here. Alex, though, always wrote to me from his school, and was an excellent brother when he was here. It was all such fun." Her face darkened. "Until my mother's accident."

"Did your father stay away then?" Georgina asked gently. Her experience of men had always been that they were seldom about when there was unpleasantness afoot.

"Not at all! My parents *loved* each other. Father never left Fair Oak after that, not even for a day, until he died. But it was much quieter here, and Alex was away at war. He wrote to us every week, but I was terribly worried about him. I felt so very alone."

Georgina reached for Emily's hand. "I am so sorry, Emily. I do know how it feels to be alone."

Emily smiled, and squeezed her hand. "I am not alone anymore, though! Alex is home again, safe. Best of all, he has brought you to us. None of us ever has to be alone again."

"No," Georgina answered slowly. "We never have to be alone again."

Chapter Seventeen

"Georgina, you have a letter!" Emily said as she sorted through the post at the breakfast table. Then she added slyly, "Alas, it is not from my brother."

Georgina laughed, and reached for her letter. "Why ever should it be from your brother, Emily?"

"Oh, I don't know. I just think he should write you again," answered Emily. "That one small note letting us know he arrived at the Grange was so paltry. Has he never sent you any *billets doux*, then, Georgina?"

"Emily!" Dorothy admonished. "That is hardly any of our business."

Emily grinned unrepentantly. "Oh. Sorry."

Dorothy grinned in return. "So," she said. "Has he, Georgina?"

Georgina laughed, choking on her bite of toast. "I am afraid not."

"Hmph," said Dorothy. "Well. That is scarce my fault. I never raised an unromantic child."

"*That* is correct," Emily said. "Who is your letter from, then, Georgina? If it is not too prying to ask."

"Not at all. It is from my friends, the Hollingsworths. Nicholas and Elizabeth."

"The people you were staying with in London?" Emily asked.

"Yes. I have been waiting to hear from them this age!" Georgina broke the seal, and quickly scanned the short missive, written hastily in Elizabeth's sprawling hand. She then read it again, alarm squeezing the very breath from her lungs. The paper trembled in her suddenly chilled fingers. "Oh, no."

"Not bad news?" Emily said quietly.

"I am—not certain. I do hope not." Georgina lowered the letter to the table, and looked up into the other women's concerned faces. "Elizabeth, you see, is in a—delicate condition. It has not been an easy time for her, I fear. And now she writes that she has had some pains, and that her physician has ordered her to bed for a few days. She says all is well now, but her husband has added a postscript, no doubt without her knowledge. Nicholas says she is *not* as well as she wishes everyone to believe!"

"How dreadful," cried Dorothy. "Your friend must be so frightened. To be in danger of losing one's child—that is the very worst."

"Yes. I am sure she is frightened, though Elizabeth would never say so. She is always so very cheerful. She would not want me to worry."

"But you do," said Emily.

Georgina nodded as she folded and unfolded the letter in her shaking hands. "Elizabeth is my very oldest friend. She is—like my own sister. She has always been by my side in my troubles; I must be by hers. I fear, my dears, that I must leave you and return to Town."

"Of course. I shall help you make the arrangements," said Emily, rising to her feet.

"Thank you, Emily, so very much! I only pray that I find all is well when I arrive there."

The town house was very quiet when Georgina at last arrived. There were no chattering voices from the drawing room, as there usually was in the afternoons—no music, no laughter. The curtains were all drawn; the butler spoke almost in a whisper.

Georgina feared for one breathless, dreadful moment that she had entered a house of mourning. That Elizabeth was gone from them.

"Greene, please," she beseeched the dour butler. "Please tell me quickly what has happened. If the worst has happened . . ."

"The worst, Mrs. Beaumont?"

"If Lady Elizabeth has—has . . ."

Before she could choke out the rest of her sentence, there was the soft sound of slippers pattering along the upstairs corridor. Elizabeth appeared at the top of the stairs, looking rather pale in her sky-blue dressing gown, but alive and whole.

Her hand rested atop the growing mound of her stomach.

"Georgie!" she cried, starting carefully down the staircase, her hands on the banister. "You are back."

"Of course I am back! Did you think I could stay away after receiving your letter?" Georgina pushed her gloves and bonnet into the butler's hands, and hurried up the stairs to Elizabeth's side. "Should you be out of bed?"

"I have been up all day," Elizabeth replied, kissing Georgina's cheek in welcome. Her shoulders felt rather thin and frail to Georgina as she hugged her. "I thought I would go insane, laying about up there all alone! I have not seen a soul except Nick all week."

"Here, let me help you down these stairs. We can sit in the drawing room, and you can tell me everything." Georgina slid her arm about Elizabeth, and guided her carefully down the rest of the stairs. "Where is Nick?"

"At Gunter's. I sent him there to fetch some pastries." Elizabeth gave a sigh of relief as she sank down onto the chaise. "I am quite famished."

"Shall I ring for some tea?" asked Georgina. "I could use some myself."

"Oh, yes, please do." Elizabeth smiled up at her. "Oh, Georgie, I am so very happy to see you! But you should not have interrupted your holiday for me. As you see, I am quite well. It was merely a twinge."

"Nicholas said it was *not* a twinge."

"That husband of mine! I told him he must not worry you."

"Of course you should 'worry me'! You are my dearest friend, Lizzie. If you are ill, I want to know about it." Georgina settled into the chair next to her chaise. "And you are not interrupting anything. Alex had to leave Fair Oak; something about an emergency at his other estate."

"He left you all alone?" Elizabeth cried.

"Hardly all alone. I was with his mother and sister, who, by the way, are quite charming. So all was well." Georgina grinned mischievously. "Though I confess, I did rather miss Alex."

Elizabeth laughed. "Of course you did! As I am sure he was desolated to leave you. Tell me more about his family, now. They must not have been such high sticklers as we feared."

"Not at all! They were very welcoming. His sister,

Lady Emily, is a very pretty girl. Just the right age to make her bow."

The tea had arrived, and Elizabeth busied herself with pouring and arranging. "Are you thinking of sponsoring her, then?"

"Perhaps. She is certainly in need of a sponsor. We would have such fun shepherding her about, you and I!" Georgina sipped thoughtfully at her tea. "But then, if she were my sister-in-law, I would be quite obliged to sponsor her, would I not?"

Elizabeth's cup clattered in its saucer. "Sister-in-law? Are you—did Wayland . . . ?"

Georgina laughed. "Oh, no! Nothing of the sort. Not yet. But I have received a few proposals in my time, as you know."

"A few?" Elizabeth snorted. "Only fifty or so."

"And thus I can tell when one is imminent. Usually. I do not think Alex took all the trouble of introducing me to his family, and kissing me in his ancestral garden, if he only meant to offer me *carte blanche*."

"Indeed not! Shall you accept?"

"I think it—very likely I shall. I have not felt at all this way in a very long time," Georgina mused. "Perhaps never. He is so . . ."

"Handsome? Brave?"

"Oh, yes! And such a divine kisser. It would be such a shame to let those things slip away simply because he is a duke and I should make a most odd duchess."

"Indeed it would be a shame! And you would not make an odd duchess, you would make a fine one. The finest in the realm!"

Georgina smiled, a bit shyly. "Do you really think so?"

"Of course I do! He will be the luckiest man in England to have you," Elizabeth said stoutly. "Oh, I feel I should be bowing and scraping, and calling you 'Your Grace'!"

Georgina giggled. "You should *not!*"

"Should not what?" Nicholas entered the drawing room just then, his arms full of boxes fragrant with cinnamon and sugar.

"Oh, darling!" Elizabeth cried. "Georgina is back, and she is to be a duchess."

"Is she indeed?" Nicholas deposited the boxes in his wife's lap, and grinned at Georgina. "Well, I did say that only the fiery La Beaumont could be a match for old Hotspur Kenton. And I was right, wasn't I?"

Elizabeth bit into a cream cake. "You are always right, darling."

Nicholas looked down at her in surprise. "I thought *you* were always the right one, Lizzie."

"Um, see, there you are. Right again."

Georgina only laughed at them.

Over the next few days, Elizabeth grew stronger and stronger. She was able to come downstairs every day, and even to accept visitors and go for short drives.

One fine, sunny afternoon, Georgina set up her easel near the tall windows of the drawing room to work on Emily's portrait. Elizabeth sat nearby, a book open on her lap. But she was fidgeting and sighing so much that it was obvious she was not reading it.

"What is amiss, Lizzie?" Georgina asked, mixing a bit of golden yellow on her palette. "Are you feeling ill again?"

"Quite the opposite!" answered Elizabeth, closing the book with a snap. "I am feeling very well again.

So well that I want to go shopping, or even to a ball. I have so much work to finish up in the studio, as well."

"You heard what the physician said. No dancing, and no standing at your easel for long periods of time."

"Yes, and Nick is quite fastidious about making certain I follow those orders. As are *you*, Georgie!"

Georgina laughed, and dipped her brush into the paint. "We only want you to be well."

"I am well! So is the baby. I can feel her kicking, as strong as ever. We both want some fun! Do you not think a small party would be all right, Georgie? If I only sat and talked?"

Georgina shrugged. "Perhaps a *small* party. Nothing that would turn into a great crush. Lady Ellersby's card party on Thursday, maybe?"

"I am sure we could persuade Nick that whist is quite unlikely to harm my health!" Elizabeth opened her book again, but she did not look down at it. "Are you not bored, Georgie? We have been so quiet here of late."

"I have not been bored at all. I am enjoying having the time to work."

"Well, it is not much like you to be so sedate! But I am very glad you are here. I should have gone quite out of my mind without your company."

The butler came into the drawing room then, a pair of cards on his silver tray. "You have callers, Lady Elizabeth."

"Oh, delightful!" cried Elizabeth. "Who is it today?"

"Hildebrand Rutherford, Viscount Garrick, and Mr. Frederick Marlow," answered Greene.

"Alex's friends!" Georgina said. She hastily put down her brushes and palette and wiped her hands on a paint-stained rag.

"Do show them in, Greene," said Elizabeth. "And have some refreshments sent in."

Georgina smoothed her hair back, and went to sit beside Elizabeth, smiling in welcome as Hildebrand and Freddie came in. Their arms were full of posies.

"We heard you were ill, Lady Elizabeth," said Hildebrand. "So we brought you these to cheer you."

"And we heard you were back from the country, Mrs. Beaumont," said Freddie. "So we brought these to welcome you."

"How very sweet!" cried Elizabeth, accepting the bouquet of pale yellow roses. "I am quite recovered now, but these are sure to make me feel even better."

Georgina took the mass of white lilies. "And I have never had such a dear welcome back! Won't you sit down, and tell us all the delicious gossip we have been missing?"

"If you will tell us how you enjoyed rusticating, Mrs. Beaumont," said Hildebrand.

"I found it delightful," answered Georgina. "The country air is so *bracing*, you know."

Freddie and Hildebrand looked at each other with matching, gleeful grins. "Oh, yes, we do know," said Freddie. "Did our friend Wayland not return to Town with you? We had not heard he was back."

"Oh, no. He had an emergency to see to at his other estate, so he left Fair Oak a few days before I did."

Freddie looked deeply disappointed. "Do you know when he means to return? Has he written to you, Mrs. Beaumont?"

"Only a note to let his mother, his sister, and me know he had arrived safely at his destination. You seem quite interested in Lord Wayland's doings, Mr. Marlow. And you, too, Lord Garrick." Georgina laughed. "Never fear, though! I am sure he will return to London soon enough."

"Well, that is a relief!" Freddie sighed. "There was that wager, you see, and I owe my tailor . . ."

Georgina's gaze sharpened as she looked at Freddie. "A wager, Mr. Marlow? Of what sort?"

Hildebrand smacked Freddie hard on his shoulder. "Now you have done it, you careless puppy!"

"Ow!" Freddie clutched at his shoulder. "Why did you do that, Hildebrand? I thought she knew of it."

Georgina set her teacup down with a clatter, and stood up, her hands planted on her hips, to loom over them. "Thought I knew about *what*? Tell me. Have I been the object of some sort of sordid speculation?"

"Georgie!" Elizabeth reached out to tug at Georgina's skirt. "My dear, do sit down. He can hardly explain with you looming over him like that."

Georgina reluctantly sat back down. "Well? Do tell, Mr. Marlow."

"It—it was not *sordid*, Mrs. Beaumont," Freddie protested. "I—or maybe it was Hildebrand—merely said that Wayland would—would offer for you before the end of the Season. That is all!" He shrank back in his chair.

Georgina pursed her lips. "I see. And what about you, Viscount Garrick?"

Hildebrand, who had been smirking over his friend's cornering, blanched. "M-me, Mrs. Beaumont?"

"What was your part in the wager?"

"I—or maybe it was Freddie—said it would take him at least a year. Or something of that sort."

"Hm. And did Lord Wayland take any part of this?"

"Oh, no! Never!" Hildebrand and Freddie chorused.

"He said we were fools to make any sort of wager on something as unpredictable as people," said Hildebrand. "And he refused to take any part of it. It was only us, Mrs. Beaumont, and I swear we are heartily sorry for it!"

"Well. At least Wayland showed some sense." Georgina looked at Elizabeth, and grinned.

They both burst into laughter, much to the shock of Hildebrand and Freddie, who stared at them open-mouthed, like landed fish.

"Oh!" gasped Georgina. "You two really are so very funny. It is no wonder that Al—Wayland likes to keep you about!"

"Funny, and dear!" Elizabeth wiped at her eyes. "You have quite brightened our day, I do declare."

Freddie and Hildebrand looked at each other, still bewildered. Then they looked back at the giggling ladies.

"Well," said Hildebrand. "I am only glad I could be of service."

"Oh, you have," said Elizabeth. "We have been quite shut away here, with nothing to amuse us for days."

"In that case, you should come with us to Vauxhall on Friday!" said Freddie.

"To Vauxhall?" said Georgina, with a prickling of interest.

"There is to be a masquerade," Hildebrand said. "Freddie and I have reserved a box, where you would be quite safe. Lady Fitzgerald and her niece are to accompany us. And your husband must come, too, Lady Elizabeth. It will be such a merry evening! You must come!"

"Oh, I should so like to," Elizabeth said wistfully.

"I have not been to a masquerade since last we were in Venice. Would you not like to, Georgina?"

"Yes, of course," said Georgina. "I adore a masquerade! But are you certain you are quite up to it, Lizzie?"

"Of course I am! I will not dance, or wander about. I will only sit in the box, and watch. It will be good for us to get out of this house."

"Wonderful, we accept your kind invitation," Georgina said. Then she added, "As long as there is no more talk of wagers!"

"Oh, no!" cried Freddie.

"Never again, Mrs. Beaumont," said Hildebrand. "We *promise.*"

Chapter Eighteen

Alex's heart was filled with excitement—and trepidation—when he at last turned down the lane that led to Fair Oak.

He had been gone for several days, trying futilely to solve the many problems at the Grange, an estate that was even more ramshackle than Fair Oak. There had been many problems indeed, and he had been busy from sunup to sundown every day.

But even all that activity, all those worries, could not erase thoughts of Georgina. They would come to him at the oddest times. As he inspected a drain, he would see her green eyes, sparkling with some mischief. As he repaired a roof, he would see her slim, pale hands, deftly wielding a piece of charcoal over an open sketchbook.

As he would drift into sleep at night, he would imagine they were dancing again, floating across a ballroom, his arms about her. He would relive their kiss in the summerhouse, just before he would fall asleep with a smile on his face.

He wondered often how she was faring with his mother and Emily. Perhaps they had given another party, or attended a *soirée* at some neighbor's home. He envisioned her walking in the gardens with Emily, or going to the shops in the village.

He also envisioned her, with a cold pang, examining the house more closely—seeing all the flaws in it, the shabby draperies, the missing artwork and ornaments. Finding it wanting; finding it not at all the sort of place she would want to live in after all.

Alex longed to see her, yet he half feared it, as well. Would she rush out to greet him, to kiss his cheek and say she had missed him? Or would she look at him with reproach, with pity?

Pity was the one thing he could never bear to see in her lovely eyes.

So deeply were his thoughts occupied with Georgina, that he was almost surprised to not see her waiting on the front steps when he turned into view of the house.

What he *did* see surprised him even more.

There were two men on his roof, clambering about with much noise of hammering and sawing. A hearty country housemaid was scrubbing at the windows, while another beat at a dusty rug hung up on a line. A rather gnarled old man was clipping efficiently at the hedges, and a younger man was clearing the brush from the neglected flower beds.

Alex had not seen so much activity about Fair Oak since before he left for Spain.

And in the midst of it all was his sister, flitting from the gardeners to the maids, giving some instructions, pulling up some weeds, pushing aside old roof tiles the workmen had thrown down. She looked like a sunbeam, a dancing sunbeam in a yellow-and-white muslin gown he recognized as one of Georgina's.

She saw him at last as he pulled the horses to a

halt, and waved at him merrily, a broad smile on her face. She hurried across the drive toward him, and he was struck by how pretty his little sister looked. It was not just the fashionable new dress: her cheeks were pink and glowing, her eyes a vivid, sparkling blue. Even her hair shimmered, a halo of shining, sun-yellow curls.

She was no longer the pale, worried young woman he had met upon his return home. She was again the Emily of their old life, who he would seize about the waist and twirl into the air, just to hear her squeals of laughter.

How had such a transformation come about in the days he had been gone?

"Alex!" she cried, only waiting for him to alight from his curricle before she threw her arms around him. "How grand it is to see you! You should have written to us that you were returning. I would have made sure this mess was tidied up!"

Alex kissed her cheek. "There was no time to write. You are looking very pretty, Em!"

"Thank you! It is the dress." Emily spun about, preening just a bit in the primrose muslin. "Is it not pretty? Georgina loaned it to me."

"Loaned?"

"Well, *gave*, I suppose, since I had to let down the hem. There is a matching bonnet, too. Was that not kind of her?"

Alex nodded slowly, a faint misgiving stirring. Georgina was *giving* his sister gowns? "Very kind. Where is Georgina, by the way?"

"Oh, I fear she is not here. She received a letter from her friend, Lady Elizabeth, saying she was not well. So Georgina went back to Town."

"Lady Elizabeth is ill?"

"Yes. But Georgina wrote just yesterday to tell us that all is well now."

"I am very glad to hear it. It seems a great many exciting things have happened in my absence." He gestured toward the activity all around them.

"Yes! Isn't it marvelous?"

"I am not certain. What is *it*?"

Emily bit her lip, obviously beginning to be concerned by his distinct lack of enthusiasm. "Let us go inside, Alex. You must be thirsty after your journey. I can send for some tea, and I will tell you all that has been happening."

"I would like that, Emily."

Even the library did not look the same as he had left it. The furniture had been pushed back so that the rug could be removed and beaten by the maid outside. The scent of polish and beeswax hung heavy in the air, and the tabletops and wooden chairs gleamed. The draperies had obviously been washed, because he could now see their forest-green color clearly, free of dust.

A small oil painting, a view of Fair Oak in a distinctive style he recognized as Georgina's, hung over the carved mantle.

"Things *have* changed while I was gone," he murmured.

"So they have." Emily sat down in an armchair before the now empty and scoured fireplace. Alex sat across from her, just as they had on that bleak afternoon when he had spoken with the lawyer.

"Tell me all that has been happening," he said.

"Well, Mary and Violet came up from the village, to help with some of the heavy cleaning that has been too long neglected. And Violet's brothers took on the roof. It has been leaking terribly, you know; the wallpaper in the gold bedchamber is quite ruined, but now that the roof has been fixed, we can go about repairing it. I have also hired on some laborers to begin the hay making in a few weeks. With that out of the way, we should have a good start on the fall plowing."

Alex listened to all this in silence, his hands opening and closing on the carved arms of his chair. It was excellent that all this had been taken care of, of course; he had been very concerned by how the damp from the leaking roof could be affecting his mother's health. But still . . . "How could you afford to fix the roof, Emily? The money I sent you from the Grange could only have covered the household expenses."

Emily fidgeted, smoothing her skirt, patting her hair. She looked at the floor, at the fireplace, anywhere but at him. "Oh, but it was so good of you to send that money, Alex! You are always such a good brother."

"And you are a good sister. But you are changing the subject. I know you are a fine manager, but how did you stretch that money so far?" He feared, though, that he already knew.

Emily's words only confirmed his fears. "Before Georgina left, she—she loaned me some funds."

"Loaned? Like your frock?"

"*Gave* me, then! But I thought—that is, I was sure, that soon enough she would be my sister, so her gift was quite proper. Was I wrong?"

Alex remained silent. So very many emotions—predominantly an anger whose force startled him, a hurt whose depth startled him even more—swirled through him that he feared to speak. He feared what he would say.

His worries had all come to pass. Georgina had been appalled by his home; appalled at his poor judg-

ment in leaving Damian to manage all and going off
to war, at leaving his family to this cruel state. Rather
than leave, as he had feared, she had pitied—which
he had feared even more.

She tried to fix all his mistakes. She used her money
to solve problems that were his alone. *His* responsibil-
ity, *his* duty, not hers. He had wanted to take care of
her, but instead she was taking care of him.

Emily watched him, her elfin face creased in worry.
She had looked so very happy in the garden. He hated
himself for killing that joy, for making her look so
pinched and worried again. He hated himself for the
things that had befallen her and their mother while
he was gone.

He hated that he could not solve things for his little
sister, as he had always mended her broken dolls and
dried her tears when she was a child. Someone else
had solved them, and that someone else was a woman
he loved. A woman whose admiration he had so
longed for.

Alex had been called a hero, had collected medals,
and been lauded by so many people. But he had never
so wanted to appear heroic in someone's eyes as he
wanted to in Georgina Beaumont's.

He wanted her love, her respect, since he so loved
and respected her. Instead, she thought him to be pitied and helped.

He was so angry. Whether at her, or himself, or
even his dead brother, he did not know. He only knew
he must *do* something about it, or he would burst
from it.

"Alex?" Emily said quietly.

Alex shook himself out of his dark haze, and looked
over at his sister. She had twisted her hands so tightly
into her skirt that she wrinkled the fine fabric.

"You *were* wrong, Em," he answered. "You should not have accepted that money, and Mrs. Beaumont was wrong to offer it. She is not to be my wife."

Emily stared at him, her mouth agape. She looked shocked and deeply wounded. More wounded than he had ever seen her. "But—you brought her here! You introduced her to the neighbors. You made her part of us. She was the most exciting person I had ever seen." Emily's lower lip trembled. "I thought she was to be my sister!"

Alex shook his head, feeling even more dismal than ever before. "It was wrong of me. I am sorry. I was mistaken."

Emily leaped to her feet, deeply agitated. "Mistaken? Sorry? It is the money, is it not? This is all my fault."

"Of course it is not your fault."

"It is! It is my fault for taking the money, for misjudging how you would react. I should have known your pride. But it is also your fault!"

"Emily, please."

Emily was beyond hearing. Her voice rose as she cried, "Yes, Alexander, your fault. For making Georgina think you were to marry her; for making me believe she was to be my sister, and that all would be well at last. I would have expected something like this from Damian, but never from you."

"Emily, calm down! Please," Alex beseeched, deeply hurt at being compared to Damian.

"No, I will not calm down! Not this time. Never again!"

With that, she burst into tears and fled the room.

Alex sat there for a long time after she left, still and numb as he listened to the sounds of the roof being repaired, of the new maids singing as they went about their duties. As he stared sightlessly at the new painting over the fireplace.

Then he slowly rose to his feet, and went out to the drive where his curricle still stood.

There was something he must do. In London.

Chapter Nineteen

Vauxhall Gardens was crowded to capacity for the masquerade. Every box was full of brightly clothed revelers, listening to Signora d'Angelo—the new Italian soprano—sing, lots of laughing, talking, getting thoroughly disguised, or making assignations for the Dark Walk.

Georgina watched it all, thoroughly enjoying the spectacle of it, as well as the company in her own box. Nicholas and Elizabeth, dressed as Harlequin and Columbine, fed each other strawberries, while the Fitzgerald ladies, an aunt and niece who could almost have been golden-haired twins, giggled over a naughty story Hildebrand and Freddie were telling. It concerned old Dowager Lady Dalrymple, her poodle, a footman, and a privy.

Even Georgina had to laugh at the story's finale, as she waved her shepherdess's crook at them admonishingly. "You two are really very silly! How Wayland ever puts up with you, I cannot say."

"It is because he is rather a humorless fellow, himself," Hildebrand answered jokingly. "He keeps us about to make him lighthearted! Would you care for some more champagne, Mrs. Beaumont?"

"Yes, please. My glass has been quite empty this age!" said Georgina. "But I have not found Wayland to be humorless. He merely has a—noble bearing. He must have been very dashing in his regimentals."

"I do wish we could have seen him before he sold his commission!" Elizabeth interjected. "He really looks so dignified and elegant, quite Caesar-like."

"You are making me jealous, my dear!" cried Nicholas. "Am I not elegant and dignified?"

"Oh, yes, darling. The most elegant and dignified man I have ever met," cooed Elizabeth.

Georgina sipped at her champagne, and smiled as she watched Elizabeth and Nicholas laughing together. "Lizzie," she said. "I am so happy you were feeling able to accompany us this evening."

"I would not miss a Vauxhall masquerade for anything! It reminds me of the night Nick and I met, in Venice. Do you remember that night, dear?" Elizabeth turned a tender look on her husband, who kissed her hand in return.

"How could I ever forget it?" he said.

Georgina looked away from the romantic scene, feeling a bit wistful. It had been many, many days since she had last seen Alex, and she had not received so much as a note from him. There had been a letter from Emily, but even that had been over a week ago, and she had scarcely mentioned her brother in its contents.

Had Georgina been mistaken, then, in Alex's regard? Had she misinterpreted his attentions?

Even as these doubts flitted through her mind, she dismissed them. Alex's glances, his kisses and embraces, had been always full of such sincere tenderness.

Hadn't they?

She *had* been sure of them at the time. But now, with him so far away and so silent, and with her surrounded by a noisy crowd so she could scarce think, she was assailed by misgivings.

Perhaps his feelings had been only of the sort that soon faded when the object of affection was gone from sight. She would not have thought Alex's feelings to be of the fickle kind, but then she had been wrong before.

Georgina looked off into the crowd, searching for something, anything, to take her mind away from these melancholy thoughts. She should not be dwelling on such things on such a lovely night. What she really needed was some distraction, some merriment!

Some more champagne.

She poured more of the golden, bubbling liquid into her glass, and sipped at it as she watched the revelers. The Italian soprano had finished her song, and dancing had commenced among the masqueraders. Georgina giggled as she watched a knight in full armor, obviously quite foxed, wobble and fall over amid great clanking. Not even his lady fair, with the help of an Egyptian prince and Henry VIII, could rouse him. The dancing went on around him.

Then she saw her friend, Lady Lonsdale, clothed as Aphrodite in flowing white gauze draperies, in a box across the way.

She seized on the escape.

"There is Harriet Lonsdale!" Georgina said. "I do believe I will go and say hello to her."

"Shall I escort you?" Freddie offered, though he

looked quite reluctant to leave the side of the younger Fitzgerald lady.

"Oh, no. Her box is just across the way, see? I shall be safe just walking over there. You all must stay here, and enjoy the last of the strawberries."

"Send Harriet my greetings," answered Elizabeth, then she went back to whispering with her husband.

Georgina gathered up her shepherdess's crook and the fluffy blue and white skirts of her costume, and slipped from the box. She skirted the dancers, who were swirling and skipping most vigorously, and dodged a strawberry seller and another shepherdess, who was leading a real sheep on a silk rope.

Unfortunately, the sheep had just done its business, and Georgina was forced to lift her skirts even higher to step over a rather nasty pile.

In order to reach the Lonsdales' box, she had to pass several entrances to quiet, more private walkways. As she walked by one, she heard a voice call her name.

"Georgina."

She paused, wondering if this was something like Emily's Queen Elizabeth again. She *had* had rather a bit too much champagne.

Then she heard it again, louder. "Georgina."

She peered down the walkway. It was very dimly lit, with only a few Chinese lanterns, but she could just make out a shadowy figure standing beneath a tree.

There was something about the figure's height, the set of his shoulders . . .

Could it be? Had her thoughts of him somehow conjured him tonight?

"Alex?" she called tentatively, stepping out of the light and into the walkway.

"Of course it is Alex. Or else were you expecting someone else to be waiting for you on a dark path?"

Georgina laughed in relief and exhilaration. Alex *was* here, at last! "Certainly not, silly man! But I have not heard from you in so long, I feared my ears were deceiving me."

He stepped into a small patch of light then.

Georgina, who had been poised to run to him and throw her arms about him, was stayed by the rather forbidding look on his face. He was all sharp planes and angles in the light and shadow, unsmiling and severe.

Georgina felt rather uncomfortably like a disobedient subaltern, about to be given a severe dressing down.

She advanced more slowly down the path, her grip tight on her crook.

"How did you know we were here at Vauxhall?" she asked.

"I called at Lady Elizabeth's house. Her butler told me you were here."

Georgina glanced at his attire. He wore black and white evening dress, not dusty travel buckskins. "You only arrived in Town today?"

"Yes. I stopped at Fair Oak, only to find that you had departed. Is Lady Elizabeth well?"

"Oh, yes. And your mother and sister?"

"Quite well also, thank you."

Georgina moistened her suddenly dry lips with the tip of her tongue. His stiff formality was quite chilling, after their delightful intimacy at Fair Oak. And puzzling, as well. She could think of nothing she might have done to cause such coldness.

She only knew she could not stand the little politenesses for another moment. She stepped a bit closer to him, close enough to smell the faint spicy scent of his soap.

"Alex," she asked boldly, "are you angry about something?"

Alex looked down at her steadily. Rather coldly, she thought.

"There was a great deal of activity going on at Fair Oak. It was quite lively, really."

"Oh?"

"Yes. My sister had hired new maids to clean the house from attics to scullery, gardeners, and men to repair the roof."

In Georgina's opinion, those refurbishments had been much needed, and not at all something to be angry about. "Did she indeed?"

"She told me that *you* had furnished the funds for those improvements," he said tightly.

If he had suddenly reached out and struck her, Georgina could not have been more shocked. "It is the money you are angry about? The money I gave Emily?"

"Did you think I would not find out about it?"

"It was hardly a secret! We did not mean to conceal it from you. Emily told me of the repairs that were quite urgently needed, and I made her a loan."

"A loan? However did you expect my sister to ever pay you back such a sum!"

"It was not a large sum!" Georgina cried, confused. "It was not so much as a ball gown."

"I suppose it was not much, to a *famous* artist. A wealthy widow." His fists clenched at his sides. "But the Kentons have no need of charity."

"I did not think of it as charity," Georgina said softly. She had thought it a gift to her future sister, an investment in her future home.

Obviously, Alex did not see it that way. In fact, it was obvious that he had never thought of Fair Oak as *her* home at all.

Not as she had dared to.

She looked away from him, to the surrounding trees and shrubberies, which were blurry from the tears swimming in her eyes. She blinked hard against them, determined not to let them fall.

"Please, Alex," she pleaded, "do not be angry . . ."

Alex had stepped back, into the shadows once more. "I am not angry," he said, his voice still a bit distant, but not so inflexible. "I merely wanted things to be made clear. I will pay the money back."

Georgina shook her head. "You do not need to do that."

"I *do* need to. You may expect the first installment within a fortnight. And now, Mrs. Beaumont, I will bid you good night. I wish you every health and happiness."

Then he seemed to melt back into the darkness, and he was gone.

Georgina, when she was certain she was alone, sank down onto the path in the puddle of her skirts. Her crook, which she had been clutching like a lifeline, clattered down beside her.

She felt numb, frozen, shocked, as if she had been left out in a blizzard.

What had just happened? She was utterly bewildered. That man, who had spoken to her so coldly about money, was *not* her Alex. He was not the man who had talked with her of her work with such interest and sensitivity, who had danced with her, walked with her. Kissed her so sweetly.

That Alex had been full of passion, of kindness and dignity.

This Alex she had seen tonight seemed rather a

scared little boy, running from a woman's gift. A woman's love. Hiding behind cold words. Words about money.

Georgina clutched at the pearls she wore at her throat, longing to tear them off and throw them at Alex's stubborn head. Didn't he *know* how fortunate he was to have her? Didn't he know what he was missing?

Georgina pressed her hand to her mouth to still her sobs. How she longed to run after him, to find him, to *make* him tell her what was truly wrong! She knew that her Alex had loved her, that something terrible was keeping him from that love now.

Yet how could she talk to him now, when she was so frozen with hurt? She could not. She would not! She just longed to bash him over the head with her crook, for his bacon-brained behavior!

Georgina took off her frilled bonnet and shook her hair free with a sigh. Love had always been so simple for her. Jack had been as open and sunny as a summer day. He had been easy to understand, since all his emotions could always be read on his handsome face. Their quarrels had always been quick and brief, ended with a sweet romp in the bedchamber.

Paolo, a man she had had a brief flirtation with in Venice, had had flashes of temper that ended as swiftly as a lightning bolt. She had always known what he was thinking, as well, because he always told it to the world. She would just laugh at his tantrums, as he would laugh at hers.

Why must love be difficult *now*, when it was so very important! More important than it had ever been before in her life.

Georgina beat her fists against her knees in frustration.

"Mrs. Beaumont?"

She looked up. Freddie stood beside her; he must have come upon her unseen, while she was wrapped in her misery.

"Are you ill?" he said, his face creased in concern.

"No," she answered, then changed her mind quickly. "Yes. I do feel a bit faint."

And indeed she did. She knew that if she were to stand up, her legs would not support her.

"Do let me help you," Freddie offered, flustered.

Georgina leaned heavily on his arm as he brought her to her feet. "Lady Elizabeth was quite worried when you could not be found."

"Elizabeth!" Georgina cried. "Is she ill? Does she need me?"

"She is well. She was just concerned for you. Here, lean on my arm, and I will see you back to the box."

"Thank you, Mr. Marlow," Georgina said, deeply grateful for his kindness, and for the solid feel of his arm holding her up. "You are a true gentleman."

Freddie blushed a deep crimson.

Elizabeth was pacing the length of the box when they arrived. "Georgie! There you are. Harriet Lonsdale said she had not seen you all evening, and I feared you had become ill." Her quick gaze took in Georgina's pale face, her trembling hands. "Oh, my dear, you *are* ill! We will go home at once."

"Yes," Georgina murmured. "Home. I do want to go home."

Later, curled up before the fire in their dressing gowns, Georgina told Elizabeth all of what had happened in that dark walkway.

"I was such a fool, Lizzie. An utter fool." Georgina

buried her face in a cushion, trying to hide her tear-swollen face.

Nothing could be hidden from her friend. Elizabeth laid her hand gently on Georgina's trembling shoulder. "You, dear? A fool? Never!"

"Yes! A fool to ever think Alex and I could make a life together, that I could be in love again. That I could make a proper duchess."

Elizabeth's hand stilled. "Was his family horrid to you, and you did not tell me the truth? Georgie, you do not need such rudesbys in your life. You are far too fine for them . . ."

Georgina shook her head. "His mother and sister were delightful. Unlike their son and brother."

"What happened, then? I fear I do not understand. Did you and Alex quarrel?"

"Yes," Georgina wailed.

"About what? You were so very happy when you left for the country. Lord Wayland adores you, I could see that!"

"*I* adored *him*. And I confess that I thought he— admired me."

"So did I, most assuredly. So did Nick. Were we so deeply mistaken, then?"

Georgina sat up, and accepted the handkerchief that Elizabeth held out to her. "I fear so. I saw him to-night, you see. He came all the way to Vauxhall just to break things off with me."

"Well!" Elizabeth huffed. "We shall sue him for breach of promise."

"Lizzie!"

"We shall. I will summon the solicitor straight away."

"Oh, Lizzie, we cannot do that. There was never

any promise to breach. He never asked me to marry him."

"He was going to! We all knew *that*. Did he not take you to meet his family? A man would not do that with a woman he wanted only for a mistress."

"Perhaps he was going to make an offer. But he did not. He will not."

"Well. Nick shall just have to call him out, then."

"Lizzie!" Georgina laughed. "No."

"We could draw some unflattering pictures of him, and sell them to the print shops."

"I like *that*."

"I thought you might. Now, will you tell me exactly what happened?"

"You know, of course, that Alex's late brother quite ruined the family's fortunes."

"I had suspected such a thing, yes. But Wayland seemed so very guileless . . ." Elizabeth's lips thinned. "Never say he *was* a fortune hunter. Oh, my dear Georgie."

Georgina laughed bitterly. "He was quite the opposite, I fear."

"What do you mean?"

"He was called away on business while I was at Fair Oak, as I told you, and I was going to stay with his family until he returned. His sister was going out to visit some tenants, so I accompanied her. Oh, Lizzie, you should have heard of the life she has been forced to live! She has been running the farm almost all on her own. I loaned her some funds, just to see her through some very necessary repairs."

"You gave money to Wayland's sister?"

"*Loaned*. Just until—well, until Alex and I were wed, and the farm could be made profitable again."

"I see. Yes. And Wayland was angry?"

Georgina gave an unladylike snort. "To say the least! He was furious when he found out. He—he accused me of trying to *buy* his family. I think he fears it will make him appear weak in front of them."

"What nonsense!" Elizabeth cried.

"Yes. I was only trying to be of some help."

"Of course you were. What did you say to him?"

"Nothing. But I *wanted* to tell him he was being a ridiculous, bacon-brained looby. Among other things. It just all happened so fast that I did not have the opportunity. More is the pity."

Elizabeth giggled. "Georgie!"

"He was not the man I imagined him to be."

"So it is well and truly over?"

"Yes."

"Deep in your heart?"

"Yes!"

"Well, then. What are you going to do now, dear?"

Georgina gave Elizabeth a rather watery smile. "I am going home. To Italy."

Chapter Twenty

Alex was deeply sorry as soon as he opened his eyes the morning after Vauxhall.

And he was not sorry only because he had consumed too much cheap brandy and now his head felt like it was being hammered at from the inside.

He was sorry because he remembered every last horrible thing he had said to Georgina.

Georgina. The woman he loved.

And look at how he had shown her that love! With harsh words, with anger over things as foolish as money and hurt pride.

Well, he had learned more in the never-ending night after he left her at Vauxhall, in the cheap taverns where he had set about becoming thoroughly foxed, than he had in a hundred schoolrooms or a thousand battlefields.

As he had sat in a dark corner with his bottle of brandy, he remembered all the things Georgina had done or said since the day he fished Lady Kate out of the river. He remembered how her green eyes had shone with quiet pride as she showed him her paintings. He remembered how she danced, so light and quick, her waist warm under his hand. He remembered how she would laugh with his sister while they played cards, when Emily had not laughed in so long.

He remembered best of all how very sweet her lips tasted.

He remembered her white, hurt face under the lanterns at Vauxhall.

And he had known, as he stumbled back to his rooms at dawn, that he was a hundred times a fool.

Georgina Beaumont was a talented, beautiful, dashing woman, who every man in London admired. Yet she had loved *him!* Alex Kenton, the crusty colonel. Not the duke. Him. What were pride and money, next to a woman like her? Next to a love like they could share?

Nothing. They were as nothing. Yet he only saw that now, when it was too late. After he had gone charging in like some hell-bent bull, bashing all the beautiful things they had together. He had crushed love, trust, and honor beneath his quick anger.

Alex groaned and buried his face in his pillow. Even that, along with the demons dancing in his skull, could not erase his misery.

He should never have gone to her when he was so exhausted from his journey, and so angry. He should have waited until he could see her again in daylight, clearheaded and rational, when he could speak to her in a calm manner.

Seeing her in the moonlight, so beautiful and radiant, had killed every vestige of a rational thought. And, he was ashamed to admit, the sight of the rich pearls at her neck had only fueled his anger.

Well, his troops had not called him Hotspur for nothing.

Now he saw so clearly what he should have done.

He should have taken her in his arms, ridiculous shepherd's crook and all, and held her so tightly she could never leave.

If she would only listen to him now, give him a chance to redeem himself, he would not care if she wrapped herself from top to toe in pearls! Or if she even papered his house in diamonds.

He did not even care if people speculated that he was a fortune hunter. He only wanted her to accept his love, and give him a chance to win her back.

He knew it would not be easy. Georgina would no doubt blister him with her redheaded temper, challenge him to a duel, run him over with her curricle. He did not care; she could do her worst, for he deserved every bit of it. And more.

But he had to try to get her to forgive him. He *had* to. His very life depended on it.

Slowly, very slowly, Alex rolled out of bed and went to pour some cold water into a basin. He judged from the quality of the light at the window that it was already late afternoon, and he had a very important call to make.

"She is not here, Lord Wayland." Elizabeth Hollingsworth's gaze was cool as she looked at Alex, where he sat across from her in her drawing room.

If Alex needed any reminders of how far and how fast he had fallen from grace, this coolness, after Elizabeth's warm friendship, would have done it neatly. However, he did *not* need any reminders. He needed to see Georgina as quickly as possible, to begin to repair the damage he had so heedlessly done.

"Not here?" he said, stunned. "Has she gone out driving, then? Or perhaps to Hookham's Library? If I could just wait for her . . ."

"I do not think that would be a good idea."

"Oh, please, Lady Elizabeth!" Alex found he was not above begging. Not any more. "I must see her. I must—must tell her how very sorry I am, how wrong I was."

"Yes. Georgina told me of your little—contretemps last night. You were very naughty."

"Then, you know how very desperate it is that I see her, talk to her."

Elizabeth sighed, and he could see her relenting. Some of the frost in her gray eyes melted as she looked at him. "I can see that you are very sorry."

"I am! More than I can say. I should never have said such things. But my blasted temper—oh. Do pardon my language, Lady Elizabeth."

She waved away his apologies. "I myself often say blast, and worse. I fear it is quite appropriate in these circumstances."

Alex felt a chill, as if a cold wind had suddenly blown down the chimney and extinguished the fire. "Has she said she hates me, then? That she will never forgive me?"

"I am sure Georgina does not hate you. But I fear that when I said she was not here, I did not mean that she was at the park or at Gunter's. She has gone back to Italy."

Alex gaped at Elizabeth. "Italy?"

"Yes. She would not be dissuaded from such a rash course, not once I assured her that my health was so improved I could have no need of her until the babe comes. Her ship left on the morning tide, and has surely cleared the Thames by now."

Alex lowered his aching head into his hands. All of the energy that hope had given him, that had kept him upright, had made him hurry to the Hollings-

worths' house, suddenly deserted him. He felt as
drained and flat as Lunardi's balloon before it was
filled. He felt old and weary.

She was gone. She was beyond his apologies, and
his love.

Or was she? He looked up, a faint hope starting
to bloom.

"I love Georgina as my own sister," Elizabeth was
saying. "But I fear she has a fierce temper, and she
often does quite rash things. Such as rush off to Italy.
I suppose that is the reason she is so very creative,
much more fine an artist than I will ever be."

"It is what I love the most about her," Alex murmured. "Her fire."

Elizabeth smiled. "Yes. I was sure you were the
man for her, despite your bad behavior last night."

Encouraged by her words, Alex said quickly, "Lady
Elizabeth, would you be so kind as to give me Georgina's direction in Italy?"

"Are you going to write to her?"

"I am going to do better than that. I am going
after her."

Elizabeth laughed merrily, and clapped her hands.
"Oh! How very romantic. She will be so surprised to
find you on her very doorstep."

"And pleased, do you think?"

"*Very* pleased, though she will not admit it at first."
Elizabeth stood, and went over to her small writing
desk, searching through the drawers until she found
what she sought. "She is in Venice, and here is her
address. No doubt she will rail at you when you first
arrive—perhaps even throw things, which she has been
known to do in the past. You must take no notice.
The storm will soon pass, and she will be very touched
that you have come so far after her. A woman cannot

help but be flattered that a man would go hundreds of miles, just to apologize and grovel! You do plan to grovel, I hope?"

"Most assuredly." Alex accepted the paper from her, and tucked it away safely in his coat pocket. That slip of paper was more valuable than gold. "I pray that you are right, that she will forgive me and accept me."

"I know that I am." Elizabeth suddenly went up on tiptoe from her petite height, and kissed his cheek. "I wish you *bonne chance*, Alex."

Alex nodded, deeply moved. "Thank you, Elizabeth. I fear I will need all your good wishes and prayers."

Georgina was deeply sorry the moment the English coast disappeared from view.

What had she done? Oh, *what* had she done!

She paced along the ship's deck, her burgundy red pelisse whipping about her in the stiff wind. She wore no hat, and long strands of hair had come loose from their pins and lashed at her eyes and cheeks. But she took no notice of the wind, or of the crew who hurried around her, or of the maid she had hired for the journey, who shivered against a wall.

Lady Kate, sheltered in a coil of rope, watched her mistress with anxious black eyes.

Whatever was she thinking of, to run off to Italy just because she was mad at Alex? Because they had had a quarrel, which had probably been just as much her fault as his?

She should have stayed to see what he would have to say, once he calmed down. *If* he ever had anything to say to her again, after that shocking scene at Vauxhall.

Georgina paused in her pacings, to lean over the

railing and look down at the water below. As if there
might be an answer to her dilemma written in the
roiling gray waves below.

There wasn't, of course. There did not seem to be
any answers anywhere—not even inside herself. She
only had the sickening feeling that she had been fool-
ishly impetuous, for the five hundredth time in her life.

Georgina sighed and sank down to sit on the coil
of rope next to Lady Kate. She had leaped without
looking, as she always did! She saw now, horribly
clear, what she should have done. She should have
understood what using her money before they were
wed would cause Alex to feel—and to do. He was
such a proud man.

Just as she was a proud woman. Too much so.

She also should have stayed in London, so they
could have talked and come to a right understanding.
This craven running away was not at all like her, and
she did not know why she had done it. Not even anger
should have made her do something so rash.

Oh, yes, you know why you did it, a tiny voice at
the back of her mind whispered. *You were afraid.*

I certainly was not! Georgina protested indignantly.

You were, the voice insisted. *And you still are. You
are afraid that you love him, and need him. You don't
want to need him.*

Of course I do not! Georgina cried silently. After
all, if she were to need someone, he could die and
leave her all alone, with the entire world shattered
about her.

Like her parents. Like Jack. Even like dear old
Mr. Beaumont.

Georgina pressed her gloved hand to her mouth.
That was it! That was what had driven her to be so
alone for so long. Fear.

Beneath all her dash, her bravado, she was scared to death. She had seized on her quarrel with Alex as an excuse to leave him, to scurry back to the safety of Italy. A desperate need to escape her love for him, her fear to lose him.

But she knew now that that was futile. Even if she never saw him again, her love for him would follow her all the rest of her days. It was a love that was stronger than any fear.

She saw that all too clearly now, when it was too late and a sea lay between them. Even if he came to call on her, he would find she had left, and he would think that she no longer cared. Perhaps he would be hurt, but eventually he would marry someone young and pretty and suitably duchess-like. He would take her to the home that should have been Georgina's, to be welcomed by the family that should have been Georgina's.

He would give her the wedding night that should have been Georgina's. He would make love to some milk-and-water miss in Georgina's very bed!

Georgina pounded her heels on the deck in consternation at the melodramatic scenario she had concocted in her mind.

Oh, what had she *done*!

Chapter Twenty-One

Venice was delighted by the return of the oh-so-dashing Signora Beaumont. And Signora Beaumont plunged into the revels of Venice with every bit of her former relish, and then some.

If that relish, that dash, was just a tiny bit forced, well, who could notice? Any hint of melancholy was hidden by exquisite new gowns, a new hairstyle, and plenty of champagne.

Bianca, the loyal Italian maid who had been with Georgina for years, had kept the Venetian house impeccably in her absence—or what passed for impeccable with Bianca, anyway. Georgina was able to move back in as if she had never been away at all.

The society of Venice, both Italian and English, welcomed her back as if she had never been away, as well. From her very first evening home, she was pulled into a whirl of balls, suppers, breakfasts, water parties, and casinos. Her old suitors were most eager to renew her acquaintance, and soon the narrow halls and small, high-ceilinged rooms of her house were filled with the color and scent of masses of flowers.

Georgina had loved this life, had relished the excitement and glitter and noise of it. She threw herself back into it, dancing and laughing as if nothing had ever happened. Every once in a while, in the midst of a merry crowd, she could even feel like nothing *had* happened. That she was the Georgina Beaumont she had been before she left for England.

But something had happened. She was not the same, and she never would be again. She had seen a new life, filled not just with the gaiety of balls, but with family and close friends. Quieter, perhaps, more respectable, certainly. It was not a life she would have thought she would crave, when she was younger and more restless.

Sometimes, in the quiet darkness of her bedchamber at night, she imagined that life. She imagined herself as mistress of Fair Oak, strolling its halls and garden paths with her husband. Lady Kate would run ahead of them, cavorting with Emily and perhaps a few golden-haired children.

She imagined presiding over suppers and balls for all the neighbors, and painting all their portraits.

She imagined long, sweet nights in the grand duke's bedchamber, in her husband's arms.

And then, still alone, she would turn her face into the pillow and cry, with the silvery light of a Venetian moon falling across her bed from the window.

This had to be the house.

Alex looked down at the address Elizabeth had given him, then back up at the house. It was quite pretty, a narrow confection of gray-pink stone, with wrought-iron balconies dotted with pots of vivid red and pink flowers. The shutters were open to the early summer day, and sheer white curtains fluttered in the light breeze.

It *looked* like Georgina's house. Elegant, warm, and artistically lovely.

Alex took a deep breath, and closed his fist tightly about the slip of paper. He had faced French hordes on battlefields, faced death by bullet or bayonet or cannon. But he had never been so terrified as he was now, about to face the woman he loved and had wronged.

He had had many hours to envision this meeting. He had replayed in his mind, over and over, their confrontation on the dark pathway at Vauxhall, until it became worse and worse every time. He berated himself for his ass-like behavior, saw again Georgina's face in the lantern light, pale and stricken and furious.

He had nearly turned and gone back to England, at the thought of what she might unleash upon him when he dared to show his face to her.

But the memory of other times, of happier moments, kept him moving steadfastly forward. If she would only smile at him again, he would gladly *walk* to Venice, and beg on his knees on her doorstep.

If only . . .

The thought of her sun-from-behind-clouds smile sustained him. Alex stepped up to the door and banged the lion head knocker.

For a long time nothing happened. The door did not open; no one appeared at any of the windows. Alex began to fear that Georgina was far from home, that perhaps she had gone instead to her lakeside villa.

Then, so abruptly that he almost fell back off the doorstep, the door was pulled open.

A small, round Italian woman stood there, her dark hair springing loose from her sheer cap. She wore a muslin apron over an extraordinary gown of carmine velvet, and held a bottle of wine in her hand.

"Si?" she said.

"I do beg your pardon, er, signora," Alex said, a bit taken aback. "Is this the home of Signora Beaumont?"

The woman's dark gaze flickered over him, taking in his traveling clothes of buckskins and a deep green greatcoat. He resisted the urge to smooth his wind-tousled hair, and wished he had taken the time to shave.

Apparently what she saw pleased her, though, because she smiled widely. "Oh, *si,* Signora Beaumont lives here. You bring a gift, no?"

Alex thought of the small box in his pocket, that held the ruby ring that had been his grandmother's. He supposed that could qualify as a gift. "No. That is, yes. I bring a gift."

"Va bene. If you give it to me, I will put it with the others."

Others? "I would prefer to present it to the lady myself. If she is at home."

The woman examined him again. "She is at home, but she is working. The Countess d'Onofrio is here for her sitting. I have been with Signora Beaumont many years, and I know better than to bother her while she is working." She winked. "You know how it is?"

Alex smiled. "Of course I would not wish to *bother* her. Perhaps I could just wait in the drawing room until she is finished. I have come a very long way to give her this gift, you see," he said cajolingly.

She glanced over her shoulder, then said, "Very well. But you might have a long wait."

It felt as if it had been an eternity already. "I do not mind."

"Hmph. Then follow me." She opened the door

wider to let him in, then shut it behind him and led him down a narrow, painting-lined corridor. "I am Bianca, by the way."

"How do you do, Bianca. I am Alexander Kenton." Somehow, he did not think it a good idea to throw his title about around here.

"Well, you may wait here, Signor Kenton." Bianca ushered him into a drawing room, and pushed the bottle of wine she held into his hand. "I was to take this to the studio, but you may have it."

Then the odd little maid was gone, closing the door behind her.

Left alone, Alex surveyed his surroundings. It was not a large room, but it was bright and airy from the many tall windows. The chairs and settees were of a light carved wood, upholstered in azure and cream. Small *objets*, boxes and figurines, were scattered on the tables; several paintings in Georgina's bold style hung on the blue-painted walls. He could also see what Bianca had meant when she said *others*. There were flowers piled along one wall, gaily wrapped parcels stacked on the pale blue carpet, letters laying unopened on the desk.

Alex laughed wryly, and turned away from the offerings to where a fire burned in the grate.

Above the fireplace of white marble hung a portrait of Georgina, a lovely work in a somewhat softer style than Georgina's own. The folds of her purple satin gown shimmered as if real; the painted smile was Georgina to the life, mischievous and merry.

Alex moved closer, and saw the "Elizabeth H" signature in the canvas's corner.

There, in that room, he felt closer to Georgina than he had in weeks. Why, he could almost smell the sweetness of her rose perfume.

He closed his eyes and inhaled deeply.

Then he heard soft footsteps in the corridor, a gentle swish of a silk skirt. He opened his eyes.

He forgot to breathe as the door slowly opened.

"Why, Alex!" Georgina cried. "You are turning quite white. Are you about to swoon?"

Georgina had scarce been able to believe her ears when Bianca had told her who was downstairs in the drawing room.

Her hand had begun to tremble, so she carefully placed her brush down on the palette. "Did you say— Kenton, Bianca?"

"*Si*. Alexander Kenton."

"Are you quite sure?"

Bianca snorted in affront. "My hearing is excellent, signora! He said he has brought you a gift, but when I said I would put it with the others, he insisted he give it to you himself."

"Did he?" A gift. Alex had come all the way from England to give her a *gift?*

The mind reeled at the thought of what it could be.

"*Si*. I have put him in the drawing room, signora, because he said he would wait for however long it took for you to finish your work."

Alex, *here!* In her very house. It only just began to sink in. Oh, how she wanted to fly down the stairs to him!

She looked over to the countess, who had been listening to them with the greatest interest.

The countess made a shooing motion with the ostrich feather fan she held. "Go, *cara*, go! I will come back another day."

"Are you certain, Countess?" Georgina said.

"*Amore* is so much more important than any old

portrait!" she answered, already stepping down from the dais where she posed. "I must be returning to my *caro sposo* now, anyway."

Georgina laughed. "Then, I will see you again on Wednesday!"

She tugged off her paint-stained smock, and looked quickly in the mirror to smooth her hair back into its ribbon bandeau, and adjust her yellow silk dress. Then she ran off down the stairs.

But as she neared the closed drawing room door, doubts again assailed her. What if he had only come to berate her again? To demand that she cease the correspondence that had been going on between her and Emily? To insist again on paying her back the blasted money?

"Don't be a goose!" she whispered to herself. "Why would he come all the way to Venice just to quarrel?"

He would not, of course. That would be silly. His presence here could only indicate something positive.

Could it not?

Georgina took a steadying breath, and reached out to push open the door before she could lose her courage.

It was indeed Alex, standing before her fireplace, looking impossibly handsome with his tousled golden brown hair and his beard-roughened jaw.

And also looking as pale as the marble he stood beside.

"Are you about to swoon?" she cried out.

Alex turned to her, his blue eyes lighting. He started toward her, but then halted abruptly, reaching out a steadying hand to the mantel.

"Certainly not," he said, his voice low and rough. "Soldiers *never* swoon, you know."

"Not even at the sight of blood?" Georgina said inanely, feeling thoroughly giddy.

"Not even then. Though I fear *this* soldier may swoon at the sight of you."

"Why? Because I look that hideous?"

Alex shook his head. "Because you look that lovely. The most beautiful sight I have ever seen."

Georgina gave a half sob, half laugh. Her heart felt so full at that moment, so overflowing with joy. Never had she felt such happiness before; she knew that when she was an old woman, lying on her deathbed, this was what she would remember. The sight of Alex, bathed in golden sunlight, his gaze beseeching and besotted as he looked at her, and the warmth of love wrapped all about them.

She raced across the room to throw her arms about his neck, clinging as if she would never let go, her tears wet on his shoulder. His own arms tightened around her, and she felt the press of his kisses in her hair.

"I thought you would *never* come!" she sobbed. "Emily wrote that you were gone to the Continent on business, and I hoped, hoped against hope, that you were coming here. But you never did!"

"I came as fast as I could, but there was a storm and I was delayed. I went to the Hollingsworths' house the very day after, but you were gone."

"I know, I was so foolish! I was frightened. I ran away." Georgina pulled away to look at him. "I will *not* run away again, I swear to you. I am sorry."

"No!" Alex protested. "I am sorry. I was the one who was such a cabbage-head. Being such an ass about the money. I am surprised that you can even think of forgiving me."

Georgina shook her head, puzzled. "I should not have given Emily that money without your knowledge. You had a right to be upset."

"No. My pride was hurt, true. I, well, I have always been so used to being the one in control. To ordering my regiment about, to having everything that is expected of me, and what I could expect of my men, known," Alex said, struggling to explain something that even he did not fully understand. "Then I came home, and I found that my brother's actions had taken away that control. I knew what was expected of me, as a son and brother and as a duke, but I did not know how to fulfill those expectations. I was so accustomed to quite another life."

Georgina nodded in understanding. "Oh, Alex. Yes, I see."

"And, in the midst of my struggle, you appeared. So beautiful and glorious, like no one I had ever known. I wanted to give you the sun and stars, but I knew I could not."

"Alex," Georgina sniffled. "You *do* give me the sun and stars. Just by being here, by speaking with me so honestly, you give me all the universe."

"I want to give you so much more. I want to give you jewels and carriages and silk carpets."

"I have all those things! I have come to discover that they are all as naught, next to you, next to what we could have together. If we can only quit berating ourselves, and give ourselves a chance."

Alex's grasp tightened on her shoulders. "Yes. That is what I have found myself, when I thought I had lost you forever because I had behaved like a fool. You gave Emily that money out of your generous heart, to help me and my family. And I was cruel to you for it, which I will regret for the rest of my life."

"No, Alex . . ."

"Yes! My ridiculous pride was wounded. But I know that pride was a foolish thing to cling to, when it had lost me you and your love." Alex let go of her shoulders, and went down on one knee before her, reaching into his coat pocket for a small box.

He opened it to reveal an exquisite ring of a deep red ruby surrounded by diamonds.

Georgina clapped her hand to her mouth, her tears flowing down her cheeks.

"I love you, Georgina Beaumont," he said, his own voice thick with tears. "So very much. Please, forgive a foolish old army man his misplaced pride. Please, marry me, and be my duchess."

Georgina removed her hand from her mouth, and choked out, "Yes. I will marry you, Alexander Kenton."

Alex slid the ring onto her finger, above the narrow gold band Mr. Beaumont had given her so long ago. Then he bent over her hand, and placed a gentle kiss there.

It was a tender scene, one Georgina had painted on many a fantastically romantic set for *Romeo and Juliet*, or *Pelleas and Melissande*, but one which she had never thought could happen to her.

It *was* happening, though. Alex's kiss was warm on her skin; the weight of the ring heavy on her finger. It *was* happening, and, for this moment, life was perfection.

Georgina knelt beside Alex, and leaned forward to press her lips against his.

"Oh, Alex," she sighed as their gentle kiss ended and her head sank to his shoulder, "what took you so long?"

He laughed, his breath gently stirring in her hair.

"I do not know. I should have asked you to marry me the very day we met, directly after I fished Lady Kate from the river. How *is* the little imp?"

"Very well, getting fat from all the extra treats Bianca feeds her! She will be delighted to see *you* again."

"As I will to see her. I never liked dogs much, but Lady Kate is quite special."

"Of course she is! She brought us together, did she not?"

They sat together on the carpet, as the shadows lengthened and the fire died, resting in full silence in each other's arms.

Eventually they moved to the settee, where Alex opened the bottle of wine Bianca had given him, and poured out two glasses of the ruby liquid.

"To my bride!" he toasted.

"Oh, no!" Georgina protested. "To *us*."

"Yes, indeed. To *us*."

Georgina sipped at the wine thoughtfully. "There is still one problem, Alex dear."

Alex leaned back against a silk cushion with a contented sigh. "Indeed? I cannot imagine what it is."

"I still have a great deal of money."

Alex laughed. "What, you mean you have not spent it all these last weeks? I promise I will not hold it against you."

"Of course I have not spent it all!" Georgina laughed in return, and nestled her head against his shoulder. She inhaled deeply of his lovely soapy, woolly scent, and smiled in contentment.

"Georgina," Alex said after a moment.

"Yes, dear?"

"I do have one condition on our union."

Georgina sat back up, and looked at him sharply,

startled out of her contented cloud. "Oh? And what might that be?"

"That no matter what the law says, your money is yours alone, to do with as you like."

"Oh." Georgina relaxed, and laughed at her own silliness. She had thought for an instant that he would say she would have to be locked up at Fair Oak for their whole married life, or something of that sort, he had sounded so serious! "Well, that sounds like a tolerable condition, I must say. What if what I like is to buy your mother some new furniture and draperies for Fair Oak? Or give your sister a grand Season?"

Alex laughed, and hugged her close. "I believe that would be acceptable!"

"And what if I like to pay for the laborers needed for the fall plowing?"

At that, he balked. "You mustn't spend your money on the farm, Georgina."

She pressed her finger to his lips. "Ah, now, you said I could spend it however I wished. We are to be a family, which means that we help each other. It is only until the farm begins to show a profit again, which could be with the next harvest. Emily says we have been having exemplary weather and growing conditions. Then I will gladly see you pay for your own equipment and improvements and new roofs."

Alex kissed her warmly and lingeringly. "Georgie! I do love you so very much. No woman ever spoke of new roofs as alluringly as you."

"You cannot possibly love me half as much as I do you," she teased.

"Twice as much, I am sure."

"No. And there is one other thing I intend to spend my money on."

"What is that?"

"The grandest, most glorious, most vulgar wedding ever!" She tilted back her head to smile up at him radiantly. "I never had a proper wedding. And, as this is the last time I intend to marry, I am going to do it right."

Epilogue

The wedding of the Duke of Wayland and Mrs. Georgina Beaumont was indeed the grandest ever seen at St. George's, Hanover Square.

All the grandes dames whose portraits Georgina had painted attended, with their most elaborate jewels at their throats and their noble husbands on their arms. Even the Prince of Wales himself was there, lodging his not inconsiderable girth into a pew next to Lady Hertford.

Lady Emily Kenton was lovely as the bride's attendant, in a gown of pale blue satin, with white rosebuds in her golden curls. She garnered many lingering glances through quizzing glasses, and soulful sighs from young bucks, even though she was not yet officially "out." But stern glances from the dowager duchess, seen in London for the first time in over a decade, quickly put paid to all unruly speculations.

Lady Isabella Everdean scattered rose petals in the bride's path, very prim and proper in her pink muslin dress, but obviously delighted, and a bit smug, to know that *she* had played an instrumental role in the meeting of the bride and bridegroom.

Her parents, the Earl of Clifton and his Spanish countess, beamed in pride as Isabella promenaded up the aisle, scattering her petals more perfectly than any other flower girl ever had before. The newborn Viscount Killingsham slept peacefully on the countess's green-velvet-covered lap.

In the very front pew sat the delighted Hollingsworths. Elizabeth could be seen distinctly wiping away copious tears of joy. Rather less moved were the newly arrived Georgina and Isobel, little angels of perfection asleep in their baskets.

The groom was attended by the Viscount Garrick and Mr. Frederick Marlow, who were still basking in their notoriety after a well-publicized "incident" at Astley's Amphitheater the week before. But they were perfectly dignified in St. George's.

The bride wore jonquil-yellow silk, with a bandeau of topaz and seed pearls in her hair. She carried a bouquet of white roses and lilies. Very striking, all agreed, and most becoming for a fourth-time bride.

The bridegroom was very handsome and most noble—if he could only have ceased *grinning* quite so much.

It was the crowning jewel of a most delightful, and eventful, Season.

Georgina and Alex, after all the ceremony and festivities were concluded, settled into the flower-bedecked carriage with Lady Kate, headed for a Scottish wedding trip.

"Oh, my darling," Georgina sighed happily. "I know that some high sticklers would not approve of weddings with babies and dogs in attendance . . ."

"Like a wedding in a nursery," Alex mimicked in a high-pitched voice, sounding just like old Lady Collins.

"Exactly!" Georgina laughed. "But I think it was the grandest wedding ever."

"My dear Lady Wayland," Alex said, leaning in to kiss his bride. "I could not agree more."

Lady Kate barked out her most hearty agreement.

Signet Regency Romances *from* Allison Lane

"A FORMIDABLE TALENT...
MS. LANE NEVER FAILS TO
DELIVER THE GOODS."
—*ROMANTIC TIMES*